SURREAL ESTATE

A NOVEL

Sugar

PRAISE FOR
SURREAL ESTATE

"Crazy rich Palm Beach! This book has it all. I was immersed in a witty and well observed world of billionaires, crooks and amazing properties. It's a page turner from the start. I can't wait to see the movie."

- Billy Williams, Film Editor's Hall of Fame 2008

"I couldn't put it down. Everyone in Palm Beach real estate is going to be searching for themselves in these hilariously drawn characters. Sugar nailed it."

- Lora Nelson, Realtor, Town and Country Real Estate, East Hampton, NY

"An uproarious, insiders look into the storied world of Palm Beach luxury real estate. No one escapes scrutiny from either side of the bridge in this clever, fast paced caper. A treat!"

- Steve Coz, Former Editor-in-Chief- *The National Enquirer*

Absorbing!

- Pushkin, Sugar's puppy

Sugar/Surreal Estate
Printed in the United States of America

This is a work of fiction. Names, characters, places, and incidents are a product of the author's imagination. Locales and public names are sometimes used for atmospheric purposes. Any resemblance to actual people, living or dead, or to businesses, companies, events, institutions, or locales is completely coincidental.

Surreal Estate/ Sugar. -- 1st ed.

ISBN 978-1727431711 Print Edition

THANK YOU NINA, STACEY & STACEY
FOR LALA

*Corruption, Greed, and **Palm Beach Real Estate***

CHAPTER 1

TERRI TRIED NOT to stare at Ursula Lurie's lips, but they were visible from every angle in the slow, mirrored elevator. They were huge. And they weren't there four days ago. Now they were in some kind of competition with Ursula's boobs. Anywhere else in the county someone would have already stabbed Ursula with an EpiPen.

"Vat is ze point? Ve are not in Palm Beach. Ve are on ze other side from ze vater," Ursula spat through her swollen lips at her husband in a German accent. Terri had to hand it to Ben. Whatever his motive, he was doing a decent job convincing Ursula this was a good place to live.

"What's wrong with this one? It's in a beautiful building, Urs, with great views. There's a doorman to carry your crap. It's perfect."

"I don't vant an apartment if it cannot be in ze Palm Beach. I don't vant an apartment at all."

C'mon Ben, don't let me down. Terri had spent two agonizing weeks with these people and was having a general real estate slump. Ben wheedled away at his forty-years-younger wife. *Go, Ben.*

"There's nothing else we can do right now. C'mon, sweet cheeks, you'll see. It won't matter. We'll come outta this alright."

Ursula was buying none of Ben's pitch. Her nostrils flared, her bosom swelled, and her lips remained fixed, though she managed to form more words.

"Alright? Alright ven? Ve are living ze nightmare."

PING.

Mercifully, the elevator arrived, and they all stepped out into the foyer before Ursula and Ben's spat could escalate into violence (like it had last week in the laundry room of Ibis Island Villa #511). Ursula had viciously pinched Ben in the neck, setting off a bout of angina that required paramedics to cart him away for a tune-up. Remarkably, Ben made it back in time for the 4:00 p.m. showing of Ibis Island Villa #523, which Ursula also hated.

Today, Terri had surprisingly been given the correct apartment key by one of the doormen. She led the Luries from the foyer into what she sincerely hoped would become their new home. It was an old, low-ceilinged, dated luxury condominium with new modern bits shellacked all over it—much like Ben and Ursula themselves. But it had a dynamite view. No hyperbole needed. You could see across the intracoastal waterway, over the island of Palm Beach, to the sapphire blue ocean beyond. Ben Lurie was all over this scene. *Go, Ben.*

"Hey, there. Hey. Look at that view. It's like a postcard. You can see all of Palm Beach and even the ocean in the background." Ursula wasn't listening. She was admiring herself in a passing mirror, so Ben *snapped* his fingers at Terri. *SNAP. SNAP.* "So, Tami—"

She took a beat to put the keys down on the counter. "It's Terri."

"So, Terri—" *SNAP.* He gestured to her feet. "You got some paper hanging off your shoe there. So, what about this place?"

Try as she might, Terri was un-neat. Even when she wore her only stiff and conservative suit, something about her was a mess. Terri was either untucked or hanging askew or misbuttoned or—as Ben Lurie pointed out—dragging toilet paper. It wasn't that Terri was dirty or had bad taste. It was that she just never looked in a mirror or thought about what she looked like beyond getting dressed in the morning (at warp speed to maximize rack time). If nothing else, Terri kept up a consistent state of dishevelment. In fact, the only fight she and her best friend, Joel, had ever had was over a pair of shoes that Terri had worn to the Palm Beach Arts and Antiques Show with him. The tan, block-heeled slides were two sizes too big, but Terri bought them anyway because she loved the little bunches of plastic cherries adorning the toes.

SHUFFLE-FWAP-CLACK-SHUFFLE-FWAP-CLACK followed with every single step.

"Terri, I'll accept this Bozo-goes-boho look you got on tonight, but if you don't stop *clacking* away, I'm going to strangle you and bury your lifeless body in the reproduction Tiffany lamp section, unless I can find an even tackier exhibit," Joel threatened.

So, Terri had knelt on the sidewalk and stuffed the toes of her shoes with wads of tissue paper from her purse and scuffed along beside Joel, trying not to *FWAP* and *CLACK*, but only succeeding in looking like she had palsy.

At the door to the convention center, the usher waved away Terri's ticket and pointed to a large sign that said: "Free Admittance for the Elderly, Veterans, and Disabled."

SHUFFLE-FWAP-CLACK.

"Uh—I swear, I'll fix it. Give me three minutes? Two? Stay." Terri pleaded with Joel and dashed off inside the convention center before he could stop laughing. She returned in two minutes, as promised, with the cherry-toed slides duct-taped to her feet.

"Ta-da." she said. Joel wasn't surprised. Terri bought clothes because they felt soft, not because they looked good or matched items she already owned. (*God forbid.*) Her hair was too much trouble to comb, and her art habit kept her paint-flecked and chalk-smudged most of the time. Still, Ben Lurie snapping his fingers at her like she was a barmaid before last call was uncalled for.

No SNAPPING without booze, Benny. Terri dutifully read aloud from the fact sheet while editorializing in her mind.

"One-of-a-kind, rare lower penthouse." *As in, not a penthouse.* "A peaceful paradise high above it all." *Like heaven. Like God's waiting room, just for you, Ben. The listing agent may want to rethink that piece too.* "Over five-thousand square feet of luxurious living space, filled with designer appliances and state-of-the-art entertainment systems." *That you'll never be able to figure out. Nope, Ben, not in this lifetime.*

But old, decrepit Ben wasn't listening. He talked right over Terri, saying, "Urs. Ursula. Sweet cheeks, you gotta see this." He'd nabbed the front door keys from the counter to open the door to the balcony. "C'mon, c'mon, Ursey. You too, Tami," he said, hustling everyone outside.

He wasn't wrong. It was a gorgeous sunset. The slender bridges connecting Palm Beach Island to the mainland looked beautiful in the golden hour light.

So did the marina thirty-one stories below, where a hundred luxury yachts waited to be deployed to ever more exotic locales, like St. Barts or Turks and Caicos.

"Look at this. Huh? Huh? What I tell ya? Not a bad view. Am I right? Huh?" Ben Lurie said this as if he was personally responsible for creating it.

"I don't vant a view," Ursula bit the words. "I vant my house in Palm Beach."

"But that's not gonna happen, now is it." Ben shouted. "I did everything I could, Ursula. And I'm not throwing good money after bad."

Ah oh. Terri cowered, inching to the far end of the balcony to get out of the fray. Anything could happen. Something else on Ursula might swell up. Ben could have a coronary. Or wet himself.

"You gave up. You are zee excuse for a man. Buy it if you vant, but I vill not live here." Ursula stormed inside the apartment. Ben was hot on her heels.

"You're my wife, Goddamn it." he bellowed after her, then slammed the balcony door closed behind him.

"Wait. Stop. No." *Who does that?* Terri dove for the door, but before she could slow its momentum, the lock fell into place with a *SNICK*.

"I'm out here. Hey." Terri shouted, bashing the glass with the palm of her hand. She shrieked after them until she was out of breath and had turned an alarming shade of purple. Ursula and Ben were too deeply engaged in their brawl to give her a second thought.

What the hell. The couple snarled and shrieked at each other all the way to the elevator. *No. No. NO.* This was terrible. Terri was trapped. She could see the keys to the balcony sitting on the counter just inside the door, which were right next to her cell phone. *Arrrrgh*. She did a tiny dance of fury. Glancing over the balcony, she noted that she wasn't even over a street—she was thirty-one stories above the intracoastal waterway. Sure, there was a small strip of lawn between the building and the intracoastal, but no one had ever set foot out there except the landscapers—on Thursday mornings. She'd have a better chance of flagging down a boat.

"Help. Hello. Can anyone hear me? *Hellloooo*." Terri continued to scream until it hurt and she was weak from the effort. She plopped herself down on the balcony floor near tears and started fiddling with her hair. Terri had a habit of twisting it up and down, and that day she'd anchored her bedraggled locks atop her head with a pen.

Eureka. Upon discovering it, Terri crafted an SOS paper airplane out of the non-penthouse fact sheet and launched it over the railing.

No one would read it. Firstly, no one would ever open it because Terri had crafted a perfectly fabulous paper airplane—too distinctly artsy to be destroyed by the type of person who would notice it in the first place. Secondly, no one would find it because it did a loop-de-loop and flew into the balcony of #5F, one building over, whose owners were on a three-month cruise. Defeated and trying not to cry, Terri pulled some ever-present chalk from her pocket and began doing what she always did in times of stress to pull herself together: she doodled. Specifically, she drew several nasty caricatures of Ursula and Ben Lurie.

Half an hour later, and after a second round of desperate shouting for help, Terri did cry. She sat on the concrete floor, sobbing. How could she be dying of thirst and have to tinkle so badly at the same time? And the stupid building was a wall of mirrored glass. Would she fry to death at sunrise? Like human bacon? On the heels of that terrifying thought, Terri began seeing what looked like an enchanted Spanish castle floating toward her. She assumed she was hallucinating some latent housing fantasy. But it turned out it was real: a spectacular jewel of a house. It dwarfed the fifty-foot tug boat towing it. And the house was definitely gliding her way. It was set up on a barge, sailing up the intracoastal waterway. By the time the glorious, castle-like house had passed from view, the sun had set and Terri had captured its detail, to scale, in chalk on the balcony floor.

The effort (thankfully) proved distracting and exhausting. Terri lay down completely and watched the headlights dance over the bridges. Perversely, it was a police car—rapidly weaving through traffic in pursuit, its sirens blaring and flashers strobing—that finally lulled Terri into an uncomfortable doze.

CHAPTER 2

DETECTIVE E. SHAY WAS ENJOYING himself. The chase had started in Wellington when a van, verified stolen, ran two traffic lights at fifty-miles-per-hour and continued east into West Palm Beach. The van driver, probably high on something, wove through traffic and barreled over the middle bridge into Palm Beach without slowing down. E. Shay was with him, smooth and easy, the whole way. He was driving a brand-new Dodge VX/hybrid squad car that came with his move to the Palm Beach County Sheriff's Department. It handled like a dream, maneuvering through the city like the world's most beautiful racetrack. All the roads were perfectly smooth and perfectly curved, devoid of potholes, trash cans, dirt, debris, construction, pedestrians, bicycles, or even cars at 10:00 p.m. on a Monday. It beat the shit out of Shay's hometown of Baltimore. He'd lived and worked there his entire life, up until two months ago, when he got an offer from the Palm Beach County Sheriff's Office. He'd only applied for the job because his last Baltimore girlfriend had become a giant tick on his neck—impossible to dislodge without drawing blood. His options were either kill her—which was incompatible with his career choice—or flee. So he chose the latter. Now, he just felt like a chump for having lived in a dump like Baltimore for so long when there were nicer places to live, like here.

Some detective you turned out to be, he thought.

For E. Shay, the chase could've gone on all night. But it didn't. The van driver unfathomably sped up a block before running out of road and smashed the stolen van headfirst into an ornate iron gate. *Shit.* What E. Shay figured was going to be a simple arrest was now going to be a long, involved drag. He was in a rotation between all the township police departments to get himself up to speed, and it had been years since he'd handled traffic accidents, so he remembered the worst part: the horrific amount of paperwork accidents entailed. E. Shay killed his siren, but not his strobes, then reached for the radio, requesting back-up and an ambulance.

He stepped out of the car and into that peculiar, post-crash stillness where all the violence has been sucked out of the atmosphere, leaving an eerie void behind. E. Shay had been here before. He had anticipated the weird vacuum and silence. Then, gradually, he began to hear his own breathing. Seconds stretched into minutes as other sounds filtered in: the hiss of the van's crushed radiator, the pounding surf, the escalating sirens from the first responders, the hum of insects suspended in the humid haze, the rustle of footsteps.

Wait.

Coming toward E. Shay like a graveyard apparition was a slim and weathered older woman. She was dressed like a Christmas present: with a bow on top of her head and what looked like flowery wrapping paper.

Huh. Guess this is how the elderly dress in Palm Beach.

"You there. What's going on here?" The apparition spoke through a locked jaw and clenched teeth. She stood defiantly before E. Shay in the billowing steam from the crumpled van, while impatiently tapping her crested, velvet-slipper-shod foot.

Christ. "Uh, I'm going to have to ask you to step back, ma'am."

They were standing just north of the crash site. E. Shay motioned for them to move across the street.

"And who are you exactly to ask me anything? This is my property. I'm Mrs. Vanessa Vaughn. This is my gate that's just been smashed to pieces and bits."

At least now E. Shay knew where she came from. The path to the beach bordered her property. She lived there. E. Shay didn't know what she was talking about "pieces and bits," since it looked to him like the gate won. The van's driver clearly lost. It would take some skill to segregate him from the van's windshield, then some more to dismantle the windshield from the gate.

"How do you do, Mrs. Vaughn? I'm County Detective E. Shay with the Wellington P.D."

"Eeshay, whom?"

"No. My name is Ethan Shay, ma'am. I go by E. Shay."

"Wellington, you say? Dear, this is Palm Beach. You have no power here. Fetch Captain Bradley."

Fetch? There was no point in explaining E. Shay's town rotation to Mrs. Vaughn or even mentioning that a county sheriff's detective outranked a captain from the Palm Beach P.D.—he just wanted to be rid of this woman.

"Yes, ma'am. I'll do that. Mrs. Vaughn, if we could make a little room here for the paramedics, my colleagues will have some questions for you." E. Shay motioned to the cops who'd just arrived to come over and take Mrs. Vaughn off his hands. They resolutely ignored him. E. Shay was stuck.

He herded Mrs. Vaughn, who was more vigorous than she looked, away from the swarming emergency responders to a place where he could get a decent shot of the crash site with his cell phone. He walked Mrs. Vaughn across the street and south of the site to where the bent-up gate had taken down a good chunk of hedgerow with it. In the moonlight, E. Shay could clearly see a wide, dirt path flanked on one side by dense jungle and on the other side by a double row of tall Florida pines. The path was well-worn and the length of a football field. It led from the road, where it used to be gated, down to the beach, where it was not.

"This side of the path belongs to Lola May, you know? You're too young to remember her, but she was a great big movie star back in the day. And there, look. Look, I say." Vanessa Vaughn pointed down the road past Lola May's estate. "There are those heathen children from the Bath & Racquet Club. Look at them. I shouldn't be the least surprised if they had something to do with this—this attack."

Attack? E. Shay thought not. *On the gate? Unlikely.*

Mrs. Vanessa Vaughn continued pointing at the three teenagers, who stumbled along the road toward the crash site in the shadow of the hedgerow. Two were boys wearing school neckties and blazers. One was a leggy blonde girl in a short, flowery dress. Drunk but determined, they weaved forward, shading their eyes from the flashing lights.

Vanessa was nattering away in E. Shay's ear when he thought he heard the kids calling, maybe chanting something like, "Kill the monster"?

Some new rap song?

Whatever the kids were saying, Vanessa Vaughn's continued orations drowned them out.

"Their parents belong to the Bath & Racquet Club, you know. Just over there. It borders the other side of Lola May's property. My mother always said those people never should have been allowed membership at the Bath & Racquet Club to begin with. And she was right. Hmm?"

What is this woman talking about?

The teens didn't register E. Shay was a cop until they had stumbled right up to him. Then they about-faced, reversing course with comical haste. Only the leggy blond stopping to vomit slowed their retreat to the Bath & Racquet Club. It was Martini Monday at the B&R and both E. Shay and Vanessa Vaughn could hear the music blaring from where they stood. E. Shay took his pictures, then escorted Vanessa Vaughn back to her own property and the crash site. Palm Beach police and emergency responders had things well in hand by then, but they kept their distance. When they did bring forms over to E. Shay to deal with, they deftly dashed away before he could try to fob Mrs. Vaughn off on them.

Guess this was no one's first meeting with Mrs. Vaughn.

E. Shay knew, regardless of how straightforward this incident was—junkie takes death-wish joyride in a stolen van—that he would spend most of the night collating, verifying, and writing it up. It was the most tedious part of beat cop work, something E. Shay had hoped he'd never be again.

CHAPTER 3

WHAT'S THIS? I'M bleeding? No, it's just drool. And red chalk. Phew. *How long have I been sleeping? And what is this rhythmic noise?* These thoughts weren't exactly racing through Terri's mind because, as a rule, she woke up slowly. Instead, they crept up on her while she levered her stiff, sweaty self into a seated position. It was an oppressively hot and humid night.

THUMP, THUMP, THUMP.

Terri turned around and saw the lights from inside the apartment. *What is that?* She clambered to her feet. The lights were from a porno movie on TV. And the thumping was from a doorman lying on the sofa, jerking off to it. His doorman cap was still on. *What?* Terri was gagging. Happy, but gagging. *This is disgusting. What do I do? Wait until he's finished? Eew.*

Marshaling herself, she hit the glass hard.

"Hey. Hey, buddy, I'm trapped out here." The guy nearly had a coronary. He fell off the couch, then tried to stand up, but his pants were around his knees and he fell ass-over-coffee-table and landed on the floor with another THUMP. To be fair, from his view inside the apartment, Terri looked like something out of a Stephen King movie, all pressed up against the glass, her hair a wild, swirling mass around her head. Her moon-silvered face was half-covered in what looked like blood. The doorman's eyes bugged out of his head. He wrestled his pants on and backed away from the window.

"What? What's the problem? Hey, c'mon. Open up." The doorman turned off the TV, the lights, and the balcony lights—presumably so Terri couldn't see him. She could see him just fine because there were enough blue-light-embellished electronics to perform brain surgery by. Terri rapped the glass again for emphasis. The doorman crept closer to the front door. "Oh, for crying out loud, I won't tell anyone. I promise. You can't leave me out here to die. I can write down that it's you." *You imbecile.* "I have chalk. See. You'll be a murder accessory." Terri shouted and bashed on the window again.

The doorman walked toward the balcony door and reluctantly opened it to let Terri in. She blew by him, grabbed up her stuff, and took off for the exit; she didn't want to be anywhere near him. When she got on the elevator—the mirrored, snail-paced elevator—he snuck in behind her just as the doors closed.

"You better not say nothing. I can say, like, you were up there havin' a party and you've done it before. Lotsa times," the doorman threatened.

Terri tried to avoid his rumpled, greasy reflection and concentrate solely on breathing through her mouth for the rest of the descent.

PING.

Terri flew out of the elevator and then, right before she reached the front doors, he shouted, "Hey, stop. You have to sign out."

Really? Really? You pervy little trespasser. Terri signed out in the appointed space:

Terri Somerville, Premium Property Partners

IN: 5:45 p.m.

OUT: 1:15 a.m.

On her way out, Terri nearly collided with Muffy Deeley: a very drunk minor and recent recipient of the Most Entitled Student award at her New England boarding school. Muffy was on a school break and was returning from Martini Monday at the Bath & Racquet Club with her parents, Beth and Brinker Deeley. Muffy would have bowled Terri over if she hadn't dropped at Terri's feet first, and had Terri not executed an amazing leaping-jog step to avoid her. Likewise, Muffy's parents never broke stride.

"Thank God that crash was fatal. We couldn't have asked for a better distraction," Mother Beth Deeley punctuated this with a hiccup. "God, Brinker, it's like Muffy's reliving our own childhoods. Can you imagine the embarrassment if everyone at the club had seen her like this? How unoriginal." Beth laughed at her own quip and wove toward the elevators.

Daddy Brinker Deeley had detoured to the front desk, flicking his head back to get a sweep of hair out of his eyes, which he did every three minutes, like he had a tic.

"Hey, sport." Brinker couldn't remember anyone's name so everyone became sport (or honey, for a woman) to him. "Look after my girl there." He pointed to his daughter, who was on her knees hurling, and then, ever cheap, Brinker handed porno doorman a whole three dollars for this chore. "Oh, and sport, who was that woman? The hot one who just left here?" Porno Doorman returned to his desk to get the logbook and show it to Brinker.

"Some dumb realtor." He pronounced "realtor" as three syllables instead of two. "She locked herself out on a balcony."

CHAPTER 4

PREMIUM PROPERTY PARTNERS held its mandatory sales meeting every Tuesday morning at eight, and it was lulling Terri right back to sleep. Sleeping was Terri's favorite activity. Twenty-six of PPP's thirty real estate agents were squished around an inadequate, oval conference table in a stiflingly warm West Palm Beach office. The agents flanking Terri, the table, and the chairback propped her up nicely as she dozed with everyone sweating around her.

At either ends of the table sat PPP's tiny, five-foot-two inch identical twin owners, with identical twin goatees, Anthony and Angelo Virga. They spoke in proportionately tiny, high-pitched voices. They wore matching bespoke dark suits and could only be told apart by their ties. They looked like mini undertakers and took everything extremely seriously. Currently, Angelo was beside himself with gravity.

"Mr. and Mrs. Lurie waited." Angelo said this with the same inflection one would say, *Mr. and Mrs. Lurie were taken hostage.* He continued, "After having taken time out of their busy schedules to look for a property, they ended up wasting three-quarters of an hour waiting for you." The agents beside Terri gave her a little shove. She jerked awake.

"Hmm—yes? What?" Her face was creased with sleep.

"You made the Luries wait. They were staring up into space, waiting." Angelo repeated.

"Um. If they were staring up up, wouldn't they have seen me?" Terri said. A couple of agents giggled.

"This is not a laughing matter, Terri. There's still that dreadful incident with the Salernos," Angelo scolded.

Oh no, this was bad. Terri wished everyone would forget about the Salernos already. It wasn't Terri's fault. Who brings their cat with them real estate shopping? Even if it was an indoor/outdoor cat? Terri had asked the Salernos to please keep him in his little cat cage unless they were inside the car, but the Salernos insisted on letting him wander outside at every house she showed them.

Every single one. There was just the one though. The first one.

Then, Anthony intervened on Terri's behalf.

"Now, Angelo, that was not Terri's fault. She didn't hire that alligator to eat the Salerno's dog."

"It was a cat," Terri corrected. "Booger. Booger, the delicious cat." Her fellow agents snickered. Angelo and Anthony got more serious and dire.

"We are not amused. Terri—everyone—remember that you are all representatives of PPP." *Snicker, snicker, snicker.* "We expect you to conduct yourselves accordingly. Angelo? I'll turn this over to you." They were like a vaudeville act in their little bow ties. When one of them sat at one end of the table, the other sprung up on the other end. *See-saw.*

"Anthony and I have gone to a lot of effort and expense this season to secure quality invitations, and we expect you all to take advantage of them."

Angelo passed a handful of fancy invitations around the table for the agents to examine. Each one was a multi-card affair, engraved and elaborately adorned: the Red Cross Ball, the Palm Beach Opera Gala, the International Society Soirée, the Rescue Polo Ponies Party.

Each invitation offered numerous opportunities to participate, from $1,000 per ticket to $15,000, $20,000, $100,000, or more for a sponsorship. Anthony and Angelo routinely bought the lesser, cheapest sponsorships available that ensured Premium Property Partners Real Estate was listed in all the promotional materials and event programs. It was smart advertising on their part, targeted toward the wealthy and emphasizing PPP's commitment to local philanthropy, even if it was entirely self-serving.

The sponsorships usually included at least one table for ten, and Terri saw there were almost a dozen of them. Terri wanted to cry. Angelo and Anthony explained (at tedious length) how each event promised golden opportunities for PPP agents to mingle with Palm Beach county's wealthiest residents and cultivate them into real estate clients. (Cultivate means "troll for customers" in real estate speak.) The charity balls were all huge crushes with half-hour waits at the bar and much longer for the valet, both coming and going. There would be congealed food, sparse drinks, dated music, and poor acoustics, and Terri dreaded attending them. June Alice, a nervous and humorless forty-something, raised her hand.

"Saturday nights, my husband and his clients take precedence over real estate business. That's the way it's always been, and I don't feel I should be penalized because you've decided to change policy."

Blow it out your ass, June Alice, Terri thought.

June Alice was one of those people who delighted in other people's misfortune and was always the first one to endorse any negative speculations. But Angelo assured her, "Not all these events are on Saturday nights, June Alice. And everyone doesn't have to attend every event. But we need to raise our profile, especially in Palm Beach."

Wee, elderly Fay, who specialized in end-of-life communities, warbled.

"Thursday nights are bridge nights at Golfing Meadows."

"Fay, you're excused," Anthony said. "The rest of you: let's make an effort. Angelo?" Anthony sat.

Angelo popped up, unfolded a newspaper, and pointed to a photograph on the front page. It showed a close-up of a crumpled van crashed into a gate with the headline: "Dead End at Vaughn May Gate," followed by two columns of copy. There was a second, aerial photograph (probably downloaded from Google Earth) that showed the crash site at the head of a path running between the Vaughn Estate and the May Estate. They were identified with arrows in the picture.

"I want to draw everyone's attention to this." Angelo pointed at the photo, then read aloud. "There was another fatal crash at the intersection of North Ocean Boulevard and the Vaughn and May Estates. The properties are separated by a gated easement to the beach." Angelo stopped reading and said, "This is news you can use people. Remember. Every obituary is an opportunity. This says ANOTHER fatality. Maybe Mr. May or Mr. Vaugh want to move to a less dangerous area? Something on a cul-du-sac? Suppose Mr. Vaughn or Mr. May were involved in the crash? Think 'Estate Sale.' We need to get out there and court these people."

If I'd wanted to chase ambulances, I'd have been a personal injury attorney, Terri thought.

"Excuse me." Joel, Terri's best friend and Premium Property Partners office manager, swanned into the conference room and interrupted the meeting. He was the type of fellow to whom swanning came naturally.

"Ya'll excuse me and forgive me. Terri, there's a representative from the May Estate holding for you on line one."

"Joe-ell?" Terri asked. Everyone was looking at her expectantly.

She had imbued her mispronunciation of Joel's name with a world of meaning—specifically, *Now's not the time to be pulling one of your pranks, Joel. I am in deep enough poop already.* Terri emphasized her telepathy with a scowl and a head shake.

Joel shrugged. "Line one."

CHAPTER 5

ANTHONY DROVE WITH his big, funereal Mercedes glued to Terri's bumper the whole way to the May Estate, like she was trying to lose him. And it had crossed her mind. After making her repeat the phone call verbatim twice, Anthony was convinced this was a legitimate Palm Beach oceanfront listing appointment: the holy grail of residential real estate, and he was determined to go with her.

Since Terri had never heard of the woman who had called her, or of the May Estate before that moment, she was pretty sure someone had found an old business card of hers for restoration and faux painting work. It was how she paid for real estate school to begin with. It was hard and tedious work she'd gladly do now for some extra money to get her over this dry spell. But not with dire, little Anthony up her bum. He would view it as interfering with being a full-time PPP agent and probably fire her. All PPP agents worked full-time. Anthony and Angelo hated the "dabblers" who sold real estate as a hobby between their tennis games and Botox appointments. Now that she was here, Terri thought maybe Anthony was right. This was not your typical Palm Beach estate. And it needed a good deal more than some faux painting. This was a mini-Amazon, complete with its own swarmy, crawly ecosystem. Terri was suddenly glad Anthony was with her. He was more Anaconda snack-sized than she was.

They got out of their cars at the impassable halfway mark up the drive and followed the twisting, narrow gravel road on foot. They shoved vines and mosquito swarms out of their way right up to the front door. Terri was surprised Anthony hadn't turned back. His shiny, little, black shoes were ruined. The house, what they could see of it, looked like a small Italian war barracks. Stone turrets and chimneys inexplicably stuck up from the top of what looked like a stone double wide trailer. Terri and Anthony were greeted at the front door by Lola May's Irish housekeeper and companion, Mrs. Irish. Really. It was she who had called Terri at the Premium Property Partners offices and asked her to come.

"Come in with ya, dearie. And who be this? Her-self won't be likin' him. Not a bit." Mrs. Irish was exactly as imagined on the phone: an older, portly Irish woman in a starched uniform, complete with a lacey cap perched on graying red curls. Without waiting for either of them to reply, Mrs. Irish lead them inside the house, where it was cool and dark. Heavy drapes were drawn across the windows inside, and Terri's heels clicked down the hall on what promised to be gorgeous, inlaid marble floors.

But it was too dim to tell. Prolific vine overgrowth obscured any light seeping in from outside. Terri and Anthony followed Mrs. Irish through the gloom to an archway that opened into the dining room.

"You be waiting here," Mrs. Irish instructed Anthony, then sat him in a sentry chair beside the archway outside of the dining room.

Ah ha, Terri thought. Maybe she'd be able to moonlight after all.

She couldn't tell much from what she'd seen, but a house like this was bound to need some faux painting or gold leafing somewhere. Mrs. Irish took Terri by the arm and escorted her into the long, narrow dining room. There were six more arches like the one Terri just walked through facing a wall of drapery, which Terri assumed covered windows. The dining table was made of exquisite rosewood that gleamed in the low lighting provided by an extraordinary wrought iron chandelier and four matching sconces, two at each end. Lola May was enthroned at the far head of the table. A silver tray bearing what looked like a pitcher of martinis and one crystal glass sat before her. She wore a gold lamé dressing gown, cat-eye sunglasses with rhinestones decorating the corners, and a fuchsia turban with an emerald the size of Terri's thumb in it.

It was 11:15 in the morning.

Mrs. Irish said, "Here be the real estate, lass: Terri Somerville with the Premier Property Partners Real Estate Company."

"My dear," Lola May said as breathily as any ingénue (though she was at least ninety-five). "That is too many pees." Terri loved her instantly. Lola patted the chair nearest hers and beckoned Terri to come sit. "You're a very pretty girl. Tell me everything." Lola May breathed and then appeared to fall into a trance.

"Mrs. May? Mrs. May?" Mrs. May was just staring into space, holding her glass halfway to her lips. "Mrs. May?" *Forget it,* Terri thought. "Um, Mrs. Irish, what's up with Mrs. May?"

"Nothing. Right as rain and lovely as ever. She's wanting you to sell her house. A true shame it is too truth be known." *O—kay.* Terri could hardly believe it. She could hear Anthony hyperventilating just outside the door. "Here be the papers dropped off by the Whitney Bank woman this very morning."

Terri took the documents from Mrs. Irish. They were in a Whitney Bank folder with Terri's name and her office number scrawled on the cover. Inside there was an ancient survey, old tax rolls, a newer document certifying the property's historic landmark status, and a listing agreement already filled out, except for the list price.

Terri read the listing agreement aloud so Anthony, and for that matter Lola May, could hear her. The gist of it was the property had to be sold within eight months or it would be foreclosed on. The Whitney Bank was owed $16 million, which had to be repaid before Terri and PPP could receive their commission. The commission would be based on the difference between $16 million and whatever sale price was achieved. Terri was confident she could do better than sixteen. She'd already run a comparative market analysis on oceanfront properties before she and Anthony left the office, just in case. Terri was elated.

"Mrs. May, I'm so happy to help you with this," she said. "I have a comparative market analysis for you here with me."

"Terri, it's fine." Anthony interrupted from the doorway. "Just let the woman sign the listing contract without distractions. Make $16 million the minimum offer."

"Does she know what she's signing?" Terri asked Mrs. Irish, who hovered at Terri's shoulder.

"Hard to say," Mrs. Irish answered. "But she likes you right enough."

"I like her too. But she doesn't seem entirely present."

"Terri, this is not our field. *No, no, no.* We do not comment on state of mind. Just let her sign the contract." Anthony was getting all dire and nervous again. "It's hardly worth our expense to list it for so short a time without you holding things up."

Anthony was full of poop. He and Angelo would kill for an oceanfront listing on Palm Beach Island. It was the Holy Grail of residential real estate. That's why Anthony was there on Terri's listing appointment to begin with. Terri knelt so she was face to face with Lola.

"Mrs. May?"

"I'm Lola, honey."

"Okay, Lola Honey." That got a laugh out of Lola. "Where will you move to? When this is gone?" Terri asked.

Anthony jumped up from his perch and stepped into the dining room. "Excellent thinking, Terri. Why bring in someone new when Mrs. May's already so comfortable with you? Take Mrs. May out and show her some properties this very afternoon." Anthony was positively trembling.

"Sit down." scolded Mrs. Irish with considerable force. "Can't ya see you're frightening Mrs. May?" Lola May was cowering in her chair and making little gasping sounds. She had a death grip on Terri's arm.

"Really, Anthony," Terri added because she could. Anthony stepped out of the room and plopped back down on his chair. Terri envisioned him with his little arms folded tightly across his chest, his little feet swinging, not quite meeting the floor.

Lola May had instantly resumed her vague demeanor with Anthony's departure.

"And what makes you think Mrs. May'd be going off with the lass when she hasn't set foot out of this house in forty-six years?"

What are the odds? Terri thought. Anthony consoled Lola May from his sentry chair. It was what he and Angelo did best, and it restored his mood greatly.

"I do apologize, Mrs. May. Rest assured, all of us at Premium Property Partners will be there for you and Mrs. Irish when that very difficult time arrives." Mrs. Irish snorted her response.

"And one more last signature here," Terri instructed Lola May.

"My name?" Lola asked.

"Yes. Your own name," Terri confirmed. "It's a great name too. Lola Honey."

Lola handed the signed listing agreement back to Terri and said, "You are sweet. But do take that unhappy little man with you when you go."

CHAPTER 6

ON THE UPSIDE, Terri was the only real estate agent at Premium Property Partners Real Estate to ever capture a prestigious oceanfront listing in Palm Beach. Mrs. May's property, albeit overgrown enough to rival the rainforests, encompassed seventy-five feet of direct Palm Beach oceanfront property, so Terri was returned to Anthony and Angelo's good graces.

Additionally, with this one listing, Terri stood to make enough money to pay off her overdue credit card bills and restock her art supplies. It was a windfall Terri desperately needed. On the down side, the owner was a stewed, agoraphobic starlet from 1958. Her house was a small and dated landmark, albeit in the middle of an otherwise prime piece of Palm Beach real estate. It needed an army of gardeners, a platoon of restorers. It needed to be scrubbed and aired and generally unshrouded. And then it needed to be marketed. The May Estate needed photos, including aerials and a virtual, online tour. It required brochures, and newspaper and magazine ads. Terri needed to host at least two broker's preview parties where all the area real estate agents would be invited to tour the house and have light refreshments. Terri already envisioned herself eating teeny Palm Beach cheese puffs from White Apron Catering. She'd had them several times at other galas and open houses; Angelo once caught her stuffing them in her purse.

Now she's more careful.

But all of this, including the cheese puffs, cost a lot of money—money Terri didn't have, and she suspected Lola May, egg-sized emerald notwithstanding, wouldn't either. Otherwise, she wouldn't be in default on her mortgage. This big outlay of cash was the reason realtors hated short listings. The realtor incurred big upfront costs, yet had only a short time to make the sale before they lost their stake entirely. Terri knew it would take a month to make Lola May's even presentable.

At 3,000 square feet, Lola May's house was barely the size of a self-respecting Palm Beach pool house. The inside was small-scaled, with narrow hallways, low door lintels, and tightly twisting staircases. Terri had kept her shoulders on a diagonal while she and Anthony toured the house, so she wouldn't get wedged in. As it was, she'd banged her head a few times. But Anthony hadn't bashed a thing. He didn't even have dust on him, while Terri had a blue knot forming on her forehead and looked like an ashtray had been dumped over her head.

"Who are the neighbors? They should be pitched right away," Anthony instructed her. Terri scrolled through her phone only to discover there was no service. No Wi-Fi. No Gs. No nothing.

She consulted a small stack of printouts she had brought along from the office instead. "There's a pedestrian easement from the road to the beach separating Lola May's estate from her neighbor to the north, a Mrs. Vanessa Vaughn—so it wouldn't expand Mrs. Vaughn's property any to buy Mrs. May's. And Mrs. May's southern border is the Bath & Racquet Club and, Anthony, those people scare me. They're rich, but they live in a time warp. They dress themselves like toddlers in brightly colored shorts and smocks, but they're grown people."

"Terri, people are people. Go there and speak to whomever about the May Estate coming on the market. Tell them it'll make a wonderful cabana or spa or something their club should have."

"That's what I'm saying, Anthony. It's a club where they like being uncomfortable and looking terrible. The food is bad. The drinks are worse. The décor is kill yourself, and yet they looove it," Terri said. Anthony gave a big sigh.

"The blasted landmark is killing this. When I think of what this property would be worth if this were a vacant, buildable lot—it's heartbreaking." Anthony's heart breaks easily. "It's not going to be an easy sale, Terri. What could this room possibly be?" he asked at one point on their tour. The room in question was small and round. A person could only stand in the very center.

"Bonus room," Terri offered. And then on the way out of it *OOPH*—Anthony bashed his little head. Finally. Terri continued "—for tiny elves?" Anthony turned around and this time banged his elbow. *Maybe not for tiny elves.* Terri didn't say this aloud. She followed Anthony down another cramped set of stairs. Honestly, Lola May's was not showing to advantage. Heavy drapes made it dark, and most of the rooms were stuffed with dust sheet-covered heaps. It didn't smell like a bed of roses either. Terri trailed Anthony outside as he forged his way through the overgrowth toward their cars.

"Make sure you put our P. P. P. signs out front and back as quick as you can," Anthony shouted as he drove off.

The words "pee pee pee" and "quick" and "can" never failed to send Terri (ever on the brink) into a fit of laughter. She was already giddy with the magnitude of this listing. So much so that she had a hammer and two Premium Property Partner's for sale signs out of her trunk and ready to go before she remembered that they were too big for Palm Beach's ridiculous codes. She needed smaller ones—another expense she could ill afford. Terri muscled the unwieldy signs back in her car, a trick in itself, and opted for a look around.

CHAPTER 7

TERRI PICKED UP a big stick and began exploring the prestigious property, as she was now the listing agent. Lola May's estate was a rectangle five times as long as it was wide. Terri hacked her way along the length of the southern boundary between Lola May's property and the Bath & Racquet Club, using her stick like a machete. Lola's overgrown jungle had attached itself to the Bath & Racquet Club's thorny, manicured hedges.

Probably teeming with snakes, Terri thought. That got her moving. But it was a struggle. Terri emerged at the east end of Lola May's property quite filthy and sweaty. She trudged on until she'd reached the white sand beach. She turned around to gaze back at Lola May's and her neighbors. To the south stood the Bath & Racquet Club, which looked like a prison with tennis courts. To the north stood Vanessa Vaughn's stately Palm Beach mansion. *It looks like a magazine cover.* Between the two properties stood Mrs. May's house. *Shit. It looks like a lump of shit.* It was completely covered in dense, woody, bramble hedges. Terri could barely see the houses' outline, even though it was centered on a spit of mown lawn containing a drained and dirty pool.

Curiously, the sun kept hitting something shiny on the house, and it wasn't the decades worth of grime-encrusted windows. Terri trudged up the sand and across the spit of mown lawn surrounding the pool to the back of Lola May's house. Terri had to dig through two feet of dead, thorny Bougainvillea to reach what was glinting in the sun. She'd taken off her jacket and used it like an oven mitt. It took surprisingly little effort to tear away clumps of roots and trailing vines.

Her excavation revealed French doors leading inside, and each door was flanked by a floor-to-ceiling column. One depicted an ancient sea battle with sirens and serpents climbing its length. Another had winged angels and cherubs cavorting through clouds. Her suit jacket was already ruined, so Terri scrubbed a little harder at the filth-covered battle scene—it was composed of inlaid marble, silver, and gold that anyone could see was wildly valuable. It was museum-quality stuff.

Terri looked up past the tops of the columns and saw the remains of an extension that probably used to be a roof. *This must have been a terraced room,* she concluded, a room that jutted out from the main structure with three hip-high walls. There would have been drapes to draw against the weather, but never any glass. The question was: were they structural or decorative? Maybe they held up the roof that's not there anymore? Either way, they were worth a lot. *Lola May ought to be able to take them with her or sell them separately, if she wants.* Terri could broker the sale. She still knew people in that world from her restoration days.

Terri also saw an old-fashioned push lawn mower unattended and idle near the north corner of the house. She called out, "Hello? Hi? Anyone around?" *Guess not.*

She was thinking about the columns, particularly since she'd just torn away the vines that had been protecting them from rot for the last half century. The vines had petrified, and now she'd re-exposed the columns to all the elements. She didn't want to accelerate the small deterioration that was already underway. Terri took a few pictures with her phone but decided there was nothing more she could do for the time being.

With a light step and burgeoning optimism, Terri crossed the rest of the width of the property and ventured back into Lola May's jungle.

She would fight her way back the length of the property from the sand to the road along the length of Lola May's northern boundary, thus making a parallel route to the path between Lola May's and the Vaughn property. It was pitch dark after stepping in from the blazing sun, and Terri was on top of the moss-covered stone shed before she even saw it.

"OOOF." *That hurt.* Then Terri looked up, and her heart stopped.

A giant man was backing out of the shed slowly. When he turned to face Terri, she saw he was, among other things, holding a machete. Terri swallowed a scream and staggered back a step.

"Oh, God. I mean—hi. I'm Terri. I'm a realtor for Mrs. May? Lola? Honey?"

Stop babbling, Terri scolded herself. *Get a grip.* But she was trembling, head to toe. *This was ridiculous,* she thought. To be this terrified in the middle of Palm Beach—in the middle of the day. Regardless, Terri kept creeping backward, trying and failing to remain normal and calm. The man lurched forward, and a lone shaft of sunlight glinted off his machete. Terri stumbled backward as fast as she could. It was like those horrible dreams where you know you have to run but you can barely move.

"I—I have permission. I'm supposed to walk around the property so when I talk to the buyers—I—I'm sorry I, I keep saying I. I not 'eye.'" Terri jabbered away. *Fuck.* In addition to a hump, one of his eyes strayed sideways. *He could eat me. Run. Run, you twit.*

Finally, Terri's body obeyed her mental castigations, so instead of waiting around to see if she'd be raped and butchered, she turned around to escape. She stumbled and clawed her way west, toward the road and civilization, bursting onto the foot path between Lola May's and the Vaughn's estates. Terri skid to a graceless halt on the dirt path, tattered and breathless and not even noticing Vanessa Vaughn and her dogs who were less than ten feet away. Vanessa Vaughn was clipping roses on her side of the path before depositing them in a wicker basket. She was wearing a tweed skirt and a kerchief tied under her chin, like Rose Kennedy.

"Hello," Mrs. Vaughn said. She had a surprisingly loud and deep voice for someone who was at least seventy-five-years-old and speaking through clenched teeth. "You must be Lola's new nurse. I'm Mrs. Vaughn. I live next door." Mrs. Vaughn's gardening gloved hand grasped Terri's limp, filthy hand in one firm, brisk shake. "Your handshake needs improvement, dear."

"It does? I'm sorry." *Where am I?* Terri thought. *If I had a radio, would it be playing Elvis?* Suddenly Terri's teeth chattered, and tears filled her eyes. "Oh, I'm sorry. Excuse me," Terri said. *WTF? Delayed adrenaline rush? I never cry. Really.* "I'm so embarrassed," she continued and stepped back so she was more in shadow.

"You're white as a sheet. Are you ill?" Mrs. Vaughn wanted to know.

Terri stammered, "I—I was walking behind the house and well, his eye—"

Understanding dawned. Vanessa said, "Hmm. Lola May didn't tell you about Herman, did she?"

"The man? With the—and the—" Terri pantomimed a toothless hunchback with a floaty eye. "No. No, she did not," Terri said.

"She's probably forgotten all about him. Frightening fellow, that

Herman, but he's completely devoted. Hmm? He was thrown away when he was just a boy, you know."

Well, no, Mrs. Vaughn. How would I know? Terri thought, but all she said was, "Thrown away?"

Mrs. Vaughn answered, "*Thrown away*, thrown away. Like rubbish. His parents left him on the roadside out by the Everglades. He was, hmm, six? Maybe seven. Almost as big as he is now and nearly starved to death too, until Old Fagus May found him. That was sixty years ago if it was a day. And, you know, he's been here ever since. It's fortunate you've met Herman. He absolutely dislikes strangers, hmm? Now you can have him put up a new gate across the head of our path."

Vanessa gestured down to where the path met Ocean Boulevard. Yellow police tape crisscrossed from post to post where the gate used to be. "The county owns this path, you know. We'd grow old waiting for them to replace the gate. What is your name, dear?"

"Terri Somerville."

"Terri? Just Terri? That's rather informal. Not Theresa? Or Theodora?"

Theodora? Ick. "Um, no?" Terri said. When Terri spoke it usually sounded like a question, especially if she was nervous.

"Terri, pull yourself together. If you haven't noticed, we're completely vulnerable now. Entirely open to the street. The dogs could rush out and be struck by cars. Any sort of criminal could wander in."

Wander in? What about Herman, who's already here?

****

Later that day, Terri returned to Lola May's with a bag of donuts. She'd dragged her best bud, Premium Property Partners office manager, Joel, with her and they were creeping, creeping ever closer to Herman's shed.

Terri whispered, "We're here. Just give me a minute—" She began taking deep calming breaths.

"Why? Why are you doing that? Why are we whispering?" Joel asked. He was not overjoyed to be wandering through this jungle. Joel's idea of wilderness was a bowling alley. He'd refused to get out of the car at all until Terri let him borrow the knee-high rain boots that lived in Terri's car for mucky property showings.

"It's just—I'm so ashamed. This is so superficial," Terri said.

"What? What's superficial?"

"Me. See, Herman: He has ears on his neck. Plus a floaty eye. And a hump."

"A hump? That's terrible. Who is Herman? I thought the seller was a silent movie starlet."

Joel wasn't following, so Terri clarified, "That's Lola. Herman is the one we need to ask to fix this gate."

"Can I have a donut?" Joel asked.

"No." Terri swatted Joel's hand. She called out to Herman slightly above a whisper, "Herman? Hello, Herman?"

****

Just after sunset, Herman glacially installed a new and substantially less-decorative iron gate across the head of the path between Vanessa Vaughn and Lola May's estates. He wore a big powdered sugar ring around his mouth.

CHAPTER 8

PARKING WAS ALWAYS a nightmare in West Palm Beach, and Terri was forced to park her ancient car several blocks from her apartment, which was located in a converted warehouse. She was dirty, exhausted, and schlepping giant "For Sale" signs when a wrecking ball swung across her path and right past her nose. It continued its trajectory beyond Terri, smashing into the side of what once was a low-rise hotel. The guys on the wrecking crew went berserk, screaming and shouting.

"Lady, what the hell is the matter with you."

"Jesus. What are you doing?"

Terri's load went flying. Her stuff was strewn over the sidewalk, the big, awkward signs hopelessly intertwined by their sharp metal stands. Terri had to bend over, ass up, in front of the whole jeering construction crew to get them untangled and picked up.

"So sorry; I'm really sorry. I couldn't see past these signs."

The foreman was livid. "You coulda been killed. Watch where you're going."

"Really sorry." *Mia culpa. Mia culpa already.* A couple of the workers even helped Terri to pick up her mess of metal. "Thank you. What's happening here?" Terri asked politely.

"Takin' the hotel down."

"Too bad. I liked it." Bad breath warmed Terri's ear.

"It was condemned—infested like." One of the workers had approached Terri from behind. "With rats and vermin." *Time to bail.* Terri walked away as fast as possible without breaking into a sprint or dropping everything.

Vile Breath stayed tight on her heels, crowding her back. Without breaking stride, Terri shuffled one of the giant signs behind her like a shield. If he stuck with her for another block, she realized, she would lead him right to her doorstep. Terri needed to do something before this got profoundly ugly, but what?

Then, like a chorus of angels, blue light washed over the street before her. Terri was so relieved she could have tinkled in her pants. She let out a breath she didn't know she held.

The police car pulled up silently beside them. It was a new Dodge VX/hybrid squad car. The driver pulsed the blue light on his roof a few times and motioned Terri's pursuer over to his car. The creep reluctantly walked over as Terri double-timed it around the block toward her building.

E. Shay was driving the new Viper, and (after scaring the snot out of Terri's creep) he caught up with her while she was keying open the door to her building. Some days, he really liked his job. He shouted out his window, "You okay?"

Terri peered over her signs and saw him. *Cute. Very cute. Arrest me.* "Yes?"

"You need to be careful when you're out alone at night," E. Shay said.

"I do?" *He's probably short. And married. With a peg leg.*

"I think you do," E. Shay said.

"Do what?" Terri knew she was staring at him like a fool. But there was something about him that didn't irk her in any way. In fact, it was the opposite.

"Need to be careful. When you're out alone."

"Oh. Okay. I can do that?" Terri said. *Twit. I sound like an imbecile.*

"Okay, have a nice night," E. Shay said while continuing to idle in front of her building. It finally occurred to Terri he was waiting for her to get safely inside, so she went in, and he drove off.

Terri reached her apartment by way of a loud, cranky freight elevator that opened directly into her loft. The light was superior situated as it was between a vacant lot and the railroad tracks. Best bud Joel famously described it as "garage couture." It was a huge, concrete space with areas of crap clumped together: art supplies, easels, paintings, and tarps clumped here. Beds, clock, clothes, shoes there. Another clump for real estate supplies and business. Another clump for kitchen, bar, food. An enormous tapestry hung randomly from the ceiling. The only other separation in Terri's loft was the bathroom. It was modern and sleek. Terri had remodeled it completely when she moved in. Under Joel's direction, of course.

Terri dropped her stuff and went directly to the freezer where she pulled out a bottle of Titos and a T-shirt. Her air conditioner barely cooled the vast space so Terri stored all the shirts and underwear she could fit inside her freezer. Terri poured herself a double vodka and changed into the frozen shirt. She grabbed a sketch pad and flopped down on her bed, knocking over the painting she'd done of the fabulous Spanish house she'd watched get tugged up the intracoastal while she was trapped outside on a balcony. Terri had titled the painting Up the River Without a Paddle and left it where it landed sideways on the floor.

However, this did not detract from the somewhat magical scene. This was due, in part, to the light, as there were three walls of knee-to-ceiling windows. This was also due, perhaps in even larger part, to Joel's art direction. Joel could make a pile of shit look like a bed of roses with fabulous art strewn everywhere. Some of it was Terri's, but there were other artist's works as well. She was a borderline art hoarder and had purchased or bartered for many pieces since college. There were prisms and mobiles and sculptures and masks. The one windowless wall was draped in silk screens and tapestries with more paintings hung over those. Since Terri refused to sell her own paintings anymore, they were beginning to pile up too. She tried to hide them from Joel because whenever he spied a new one he became enraged at Timothy all over again, thus making her become enraged at Tim all over again. And, before they knew it, they'd dredged up the whole wretched, infuriating ordeal yet again. Terri just wanted it to evaporate from her memory.

Timothy was Terri's ex-husband: a British charlatan and art dealer twenty years her senior. Timothy stole more than a hundred thousand dollars from Terri, twenty of her paintings, and all of her confidence.

Over the course of their unfortunate, four-year marriage, Timothy had Terri convinced her paintings were pathetically amateurish. He'd convinced her he'd never sold one of her paintings for more than four hundred dollars. He told her he often lied about the tiny pittance they garnered to spare her feelings.

Joel was convinced this was bald-faced lies. He'd seen Terri's work. Her paintings probably sold for thousands, not hundreds, and Timothy had been pocketing the difference for years. Tim's coup de grâce came right before Terri's first solo show. It was his idea and Timothy, who was rarely in town because he had so many other artist's works he needed to promote, had arranged the show and every detail. He had encouraged Terri to produce as many paintings as possible to make up for their comparatively small price tags. When Terri proudly revealed her collection of twenty paintings to him a week before the show was scheduled to open, Timothy cancelled it.

"Darling these paintings reek of 'hobby,'" he told Terri. "They're embarrassing and pedestrian. I'll have to sell them off quietly at some street fair, so as not to ruin my own reputation." He then added that they'd be lucky to get the price of the canvas back and Terri should stick to restoring furniture, like when they'd first met. Then Timothy cleaned out their joint bank account, took all her paintings, and left town (never to be heard from again—except for his creditors, including two bookies who scared Terri so badly she went into debt paying them off.) That was three years ago, and Terri still hadn't dug herself completely out of the financial hole he had left her in.

Terri sipped and doodled, doodled and sipped. She sketched a portrait of the cute cop framed in the window of his Dodge VX/ hybrid, then crumpled it up and tossed it into a growing heap of crumpled sketches located across the room. She drew a picture of a wrecking ball at the point of impact against a building. She added rats fleeing the crumbling edifice and wrote across it: "INFESTED."

It crossed her mind that if Lola's house was infested, it would necessarily have to be torn down, but Terri had seen no signs of termites or other pests at Lola May's. She needed to stop fantasizing about what the property would be worth without the house on it and get on with making Lola May's home look as valuable as possible without incurring a ton of expenses. She'd already filled two sketchbooks with ideas for tarting the place up, almost cash-free, if you excluded her own and Joel's slave labor.

Joel did not yet know about this.

CHAPTER 9

VANESSA VAUGHN DROVE her golden retrievers in a vintage, wood-sided, station wagon (unironically) home from the vets. She'd driven the long way around to avoid the Palm Beach afternoon traffic. The après-golf and tennis set had a nice post-lunch buzz on, and they drove around with extreme leisure, slowly weaving and often fading to complete stops for short naps mid-block. Vanessa was driving along apace when she slammed her brakes on in disbelief. She had come abreast of the path between her property and Lola May's. Vanessa could see straight down the path to the beach. There was no gate at all.

****

That same night, Terri stood in the open doorway to Lola May's dining room. She was on her way to one of the Premium Property Partners charity balls, wearing an ugly bridesmaid gown. It was the only gown Terri owned, and it went poorly with her yellow Morton's Salt rain slicker.

Over the past week, it had become clear Lola May wasn't concerned with things like weekends or daylight. And just as well. It was taking every free minute Terri had to get Lola's house into showing condition. If she'd been billing for her restoration hours, she wouldn't even need to sell real estate, but Terri wasn't there that Saturday night to faux paint a hallway or gold leaf a fresco. She was hoping to coax Lola outside to see the columns.

Maybe Lola would feel less terrified at night?

To date, Lola May had let Terri do everything she'd wanted to do to get the house ready for showings. Mrs. Irish had been invaluable and Herman, to the best of his abilities, had pitchforked right in. Terri stood in the open dining room doorway.

The bougainvillea had been cut away, leaving a large canopy dense and wide enough to keep Terri from getting rained upon.

Terri coaxed.

"They're like—buried treasure." This got a rise out of Lola May.

"Treasure? I do love a treasure hunt," Lola May drawled breathily.

"Well—the coast is clear," Terri said. Lola stood up from her throne, really that's what it was, at the head of the dining room table and walked halfway to Terri, then stopped.

"It's so far," Lola said. Mrs. Irish also cajoled.

"*Ach*, it's just round the other side of the doors. Go on with you." Lola took one tiny step toward the open door while she worried the nine-foot-long chiffon scarf trailing from her neck.

Mrs. Irish said, "If the lass can fetch more money for yourself out of this house, it's all to the good then." The past week also revealed how dire Lola May's situation was. The mortgage wasn't Lola May's only debt held by Whitney Bank.

Lola began dancing in place and humming to herself, so Terri asked Mrs. Irish, "How will we get her out of here when the time really comes?"

"Sedatives, dearie," said Mrs. Irish.

There was a loud rapping at the front door, followed by a man's voice.

"Knock. Knock. Hello?"

This sent Lola scurrying to the safety of her throne. She sat down, curled her legs beneath her, and began trembling. *Damn it.* Terri thought. *Lola was so close. And who was coming here at this hour on a Saturday night anyway? The dumbass just wrecked all Terri's progress.* Terri could hear that that he'd pushed the front door open and was walking through Lola's foyer.

"Hello. Anyone home?" he called again.

The nerve. Terri sprinted to intercept him in the hall. There he stood.

A six-foot man. 230 pounds of baby fat stuffed into a Brooks Brothers suit. His neck and his nose were a bright, alcoholic red above a pink and green tie. His hair was cut so that a hank of it fell over one eye, and he shook his head to flick it back. Somewhere along the way, some blind girlfriend must have told him it was sexy because he flicked every ninety seconds or so, like he was dodging flies.

He stepped much too close to Terri and shoved a damp, pudgy hand at her. "Brinker Deeley. The Deeley Cavit Realty Group."

Terri could smelled gin on his breath. "Hi. Terri Somerville."

Brinker tried to peer around Terri. "The pleasure's all mine."

"It is," Terri agreed.

"I assume Lola May's in there?"

"She's not receiving visitors right now, and she already has a realtor. Me. Premium Property Partners Real Estate," Terri said.

"Oh really? You?" Brinker Deeley said. He made a big deal of being surprised at this news. The bridesmaid dress must have thrown him off.

"In that case, I'll get right to it. I have a buyer with an offer."

What?

"It's not even on the market yet," Terri told him. Her signs were still at the sign makers' store, waiting to be picked up. Terri considered leaving them there forever. They were way too tiny to read and would cost $425 bucks she didn't have.

"Let's not pretend here. This property has limited value. That said, multi-million dollar buyers aren't exactly thick on the ground, and my buyer, who's buying anonymously through a trust by the way, is pressed for time. Here's the contract. It's perfectly fair."

Maybe this was the way they did real estate business on Palm Beach? You didn't have to advertise. You didn't list in a multiple listing service. Realtors just showed up with offers. Terri was astounded. Brinker handed Terri a large envelope he'd whipped out of his breast pocket.

She didn't want to accept anything that had been that close to his body, but an offer was an offer. "Alright."

"Go ahead; open it. You can go through it with Old Lady May tonight, and I'll pick it up in the morning. Or, if it's more convenient, I can pick it up at your house tonight." *FLICK, FLICK* went the hair; then Brinker winked at her.

Ass.

Terri sat under a dim sconce in the gloomy foyer, reading the offer. It seemed Lola May's mortgage woes were not a secret.

This offer covered it and no more, but Terri knew she could do better.

"Honey, you do know it's landmarked, don't ya?" *FLICK.* "You can't seriously expect to get more." Brinker Deeley stood over Terri making "look around you" gestures between head flicks. Though progress had been made at Lola May's, it was still spooky and cramped inside.

"Forget it," said Terri. "It's not even officially on the market."

"To its great advantage. What are you going to do? Paint it? Get it pressure washed? Stage the shit out of it?" That's exactly what Terri had been thinking. She had to keep herself from flinching at Brinker's words. "God knows you'd be a fool to do brochures or print ads. You'd be spending money you'll never get back. You won't get any higher offers."

"Some other buyer could want this," Terri defended. *A tiny buyer,* she thought. "I haven't even listed it and yet here *you* are. The offer's declined," Terri said.

"Honey, you know that's illegal," Brinker shot back. "You have to present this to your seller." *FLICK.* Terri walked down the hall to the dining room archway and shouted in, "Mrs. May, I've got an offer on your house. They'll pay you exactly what you owe the bank. Will you accept?"

Lola looked up from her throne at the head of the table. Mrs. Irish had calmed her down with a martini and a cigarette, which she was smoking through a long cigarette holder.

"Sugarplum, I don't know. I'm afraid," Lola gave a breathy, southern drawl.

"What are you afraid of?" Terri asked.

"I'm afraid your jacket doesn't match your gown," Lola answered her in all earnestness.

"Me too," Terri told her before walking back to Brinker. "She said no." Brinker snatched the contract out of Terri's hand with a huffier *FLICK.*

"Honey, if you want to play hard to get with me, I'll play. The price won't go up, but I could get my buyer to tack on a hefty commission for you. We'll get together soon and work out how big. I'll call you." Brinker *FLICKED* with a wink, looking like he'd been caught mid-spasm, before waddling to the door and letting himself out. Terri was used to mild sexual harassment at work. Even so, Brinker Deeley was super smarmy.

Mrs. Irish, who'd been hovering in the dining room doorway, eavesdropping, said, "I forgot to tell you a card's come 'round," and handed Terri a note card.

The stock was heavy with a "V" engraved at the top.

****

It was full dark and drizzling outside, and Terri's yellow slicker wasn't giving the bridesmaid gown beneath it much protection as she stood at the head of the path and watched Herman install a gate at the speed of evolution. Her hair was ringing wet.

And face it, Herman still made her nervous. He was not happy about doing this chore again and was extremely defensive about his original handiwork. Terri cajoled Herman, "I—I believe you. I swear I do. I'm sure you put the gate back across the path. It's, it's that scary Vaughn woman from next door who said the gate's not up. I concede it's not up, but—but you'll put it up again? Even better than before because that's just the kind of guy you are, Herman. A can-do guy."

Herman was flattered and smiled his best smile, which was much scarier than his not-smiling. Herman said, "Can-Do Guh."

"Right. Can-Do Guy, Herman. That's you." Terri's slicker had formed a gutter in the back, directing a steady drizzle inside her raincoat, down her back, and into her underpants. It felt gross.

"Herman, you don't need me hanging around here anymore. Right?"

Herman scowled at Terri and shook his head. *Best not test these waters right now. All alone in the dark of night,* Terri thought. Terri stayed with Herman until he'd almost finished the job and had only to return his tools to his toolbox. It had been another wet, sticky hour and a half before she left Herman still at it and caught up with Anthony and Angelo at the ball.

The dapper and dire Virga Brothers had been working the room all night: chatting up VIPs, twinning. It's a weird fact that most people get a big kick out of seeing twins, like seeing a matched set of dogs, especially cute ones, all dressed up. And Angelo and Anthony were adorable in their matching, tiny, Tom Ford tuxes. Terri knew they dressed identically on purpose so they could hit on the same people twice. Or, if they drank too much, they could blame it on their brother. Now, they were crisscrossing the room with long, ingratiating goodbyes. Terri intercepted them between tables of exiting guests.

"Nice of you to join us, Terri. It's over. You've missed the whole event. What are you wearing?" either Angelo or Anthony asked.

"Aren't you hot?" asked the other.

"Yes." Terri said and quickly removed her yellow slicker, revealing the dress beneath. "Thanks. That's so much better."

"It's not better," gasped Anthony/Angelo. Terri's gown was not looking good. But it was midnight. Who was sober? Over Anthony/Angelo's shoulder, Terri spied Vanessa Vaughn heading right toward her through the exiting crowd.

Oh, please don't see me. Terri prayed and crouched down trying to hide herself behind teeny Anthony and Angelo. Combined, they were about the size of a standard dishwasher.

"What are you doing? Anthony, what is she doing?"

"Stop that. Stand up. Stand up."

Oh shit. Caught. Vanessa Vaughn strode right up to Terri.

"Nurse Terri, whatever are you doing here? Surely you haven't brought Lola May."

"No?" Terri said, automatically.

"Did you get my letter?" Vanessa asked, but before Terri could answer Angelo was introducing himself.

"Angelo Virga, Premium Property Partners. How do you do?"

"I do well. If you'll excuse me, I'm speaking with Nurse Terri." *Ouch.* Terri experienced a glimmer of affection for Mrs. Vaughn in that moment. "I hope you're not shirking your responsibilities by coming here." It was a faint glimmer.

"No?" Terri said.

"You received my note, dear? Have you spoken with Herman? Hmm? Is the gate restored, or will we be worrying about burglars all night long?"

"Ah, no? Yes? Look, Mrs. Vaughn, I'm not a nurse. I'm a real estate agent. I'm trying to sell Mrs. May's house."

"Not to me, you're not. I have too much property as it is. And that horrible, horrible path runs between our estates."

"Horrible, horrible," sounded like "horrivle, horrivle," with her teeth clenched.

Terri said. "Horrivle path or not, someone's going to buy it. Maybe another movie star? Or a reality star? A Kardashian—or—er a Trump."

Despite Vanessa's curt dismissal, Angelo and Anthony had remained lurking and listening. "Terri." Anthony scolded. "Mrs. Vaughn, please excuse Terri. She's an excellent realtor. Just a tad exuberant."

Vanessa Vaughn replied in her customary lockjaw, "Exuberance is always vulgar—and the product of having too little demand on one's time. It's the trouble with today's young people," Vanessa announced this to a sea of drunk and bejeweled party guests in $800 shoes.

And those were the men.

Angelo couldn't agree fast enough, "Anthony and I were just re-marking on that very thing." *And I'm made of cheese,* Terri thought, but Vanessa hadn't finished. She turned back to Terri.

"You should involve yourself, dear. Volunteer. Join some committees."

No, no, no. Terri could see where this was going. Bloody commit-tees. She'd known if she attended tonight it would turn out badly. Not this badly, of course, and now Anthony and Angelo's little eyes were all lit up. *I'm not doing this.* Terri vowed.

"I can't," Terri blurted. "I—I laugh inappropriately." Vanessa spoke as if Terri hadn't spoken.

"I know of several organizations that need dedicated young peo-ple to volunteer. Hmm? I'll arrange it."

CHAPTER 10

THE RAIN HAD stopped and Herman, thoroughly drenched, was latching the replacement gate when a police car pulled over and stopped. Foregoing flashers, the two officers got out of their car, carrying high-powered flashlights. It took a minute for them to spot Herman standing motionless by the gate, but the second they saw him, their guns came out.

"Freeze. Get your hands up."

Herman cowered backward, holding up his arms to hide his face as best he could. The hump made it tough.

"Jesus Christ." Even the cops were wincing.

"Poor bastard," one of them said. They holstered their guns while approaching Herman with extreme caution.

****

The West Palm Beach Downtown Police Station was an unadorned, block long, block wide bunker with seven stories. It was as unwelcoming on the inside as it was on the outside. Terri still wore the hideous gown and yellow slicker, and Vanessa Vaughn wore a raincoat with matching pressed slacks, kerchief, and gardening boots—all circa 1959. They stood before the front desk sergeant, separated by Plexiglass.

Behind Vanessa and Terri were a steady stream of what looked like addicts, drunks, crazy people, and an overwhelming number of horribly unfortunate souls entering the West Palm Beach Central Police Station. Vanessa Vaughn was indignant.

"What?" she demanded of the portly desk sergeant. He gave Vanessa another long-suffering sigh, clearly low on patience.

"I'm reading to you from the report, ma'am." He read, "'Obstructing access to government property.' That's what it says. Look, you can either bail him out or leave him. I don't care. But the charge is obstruction of government property."

"Impossible. That's impossible. There's always been a gate to that path. Recently it was smashed into by a truck of some sort. Terrible crash, you know, and the gate was just irreparable. So, you see, Herman was simply replacing it," Vanessa Vaughn insisted.

"Well, ma'am, Herman can't. As per ordinance—" he read off a written report "C-43-8-2-2-P, as in 'Pest.'"

Vanessa was incensed. "I've never heard of this ordinance. Since when has there been this ordinance?"

The desk sergeant searched his report. "Says here, ten weeks ago. Huh." Even he seemed surprised. Vanessa suddenly ran out of steam at this baffling turn of events.

"This is simply too much. I can't address this in the middle of the night. Where do I pay, hmm?" Vanessa asked.

The desk sergeant pointed and gave Vanessa instructions. She thanked him "so much" and gave Terri a firm shove. Terri had been leaning against the police station wall, asleep, and awoke with a graceless start.

"What?" Terri wondered, disoriented.

Vanessa trotted down the hall and called back to Terri, "Are you coming? You need to keep up. Why are you here?" Terri caught up with Vanessa at the cashier's booth and explained that Mrs. Irish had called her. The cashier's booth had a bulletproof window with a slot open to the hall. Vanessa gave an impatient rap on the glass. "Hello. Cashier?" Vanessa waited until she had his full attention before carefully writing and recording a check for Herman's release. She shoved it through the slot. The cashier returned a copy of the receipt.

"Take this copy to the third office down that hall, and they'll give you a copy of the violation report. And take this." He shoved another paper through the slot at Vanessa, saying, "Go through those double doors there. You got to ring a bell. Give 'em this, and they'll bring you—" he scanned the paper. "Herman."

Vanessa thanked the cashier "so much" and handed the last paper to Terri. "Take this paper and go collect Herman through those doors. Ring the bell. We'll meet back here. Hmm?"

Maybe Vanessa was in the army? Terri wondered as Vanessa strode off to find the designated office.

Terri had walked to the double doors and rang the bell, just as Detective E. Shay opened the doors and stepped out.

******

There stood Terri in a lobster fishing rain coat and wet gown. He wondered with real dismay why he was always attracted to the crazy ones. Terri's eyes got very wide and very blue when she recognized Shay. *What's up with that?* E. Shay thought to himself, though he knew he was already doomed.

"Wow," Terri said. "You. Hi." *No peg.*

"Hi," E. Shay said. Terri smiled at him like a loon, then remembered the form she held and handed it to him.

"You're here to collect," he read aloud, "Herman?"

"Yes—?" Terri was doing her nervous question thing.

E. Shay asked, "He the big guy? With the, um—" E Shea could think of no politically correct way to describe Herman.

"With the hump? That's him." Terri supplied like a game show contestant.

"Did you come here alone?"

"Yes." said Terri, like she'd won a Maytag freezer. "Yes. But Lola's neighbor is here with me too."

E. Shay could feel himself grinning back at Terri like an idiot, but he couldn't help it. "All right. Is she coming back?" E. Shay asked.

"Yes."

"I'm sorry. I don't know your name?"

"Terri."

"Terri, okay. I'm Detective E. Shay. I want to ask you some questions before we release Herman?"

"Okay?"

"Please answer me truthfully."

"Okay."

"Because if you're afraid of something, or someone, we can take care of you." *I. Me. I can take care of you.*

"Great." *Why don't you ask me these questions over dinner? Or breakfast?*

"Are you being forced in any way to do this tonight?" E. Shay asked.

Terri considered this. "It wasn't on the top of my list. It was more like A: Sleep. B. Sleep. Around Y: Bail Herman out of prison. Z would be eat mice."

Vanessa returned. "What is so amusing?" she demanded, but didn't wait for an answer. "I know you. You're that detective."

"Yes, ma'am. Detective E. Shay."

"What have you done with Herman, hmm?"

"He'll be right out. I didn't know he was with you. It seemed better not to release him to Terri alone." Vanessa raised a brow at his "Terri."

"Of course it's better. Anyone can tell the man's not right." Even when Vanessa was kind, she was awful.

E. Shay pressed a red button on the wall. A moment later, Herman was escorted out from behind electronically locked double doors by a nervous young cop. Herman emitted soft bellows and slowly swooped his head from side to side.

"Herman. Herman, it's me, Mrs. Vaughn from next door. We're going home now. Do you understand?"

Herman wasn't the only one who cowered back from Vanessa Vaughn. Then he spied Terri. Slowly and painfully, because of the hump, he raised his arm and pointed accusingly in her direction. Shay and the young cop drew their weapons.

Enunciating as best he could, Herman said, "Ca-an do."

Oh no, Terri thought. "Herman, I'm so sorry. I didn't know you couldn't do."

Shit.

CHAPTER 11

LOLA MAY'S HOUSE was improving daily. Thus far, the inside had been scrubbed to within an inch of its life. The rugs and drapes had been beaten to near death and aired. The marble floors, chandeliers, sconces, and the paned-and-stained glassed windows all gleamed and sparkled. There were dustsheet-covered heaps still clogging here and there, but thankfully Terri had Joel to sort that out for her. He had a fledgling interior design business that made just little enough to keep him working as office manager at PPP. He staged almost everyone's listings for a modest fee at closing but went far above and beyond for Terri. So far Joel's instructions were to "clean and sterilize everything, but throw nothing away."

Terri had unearthed several treasures but nothing to rival the eight decorative columns outside the dining room doors. She was out there now, examining the newly revealed east façade of Lola May's house. It really was incredible how well they had been protected all these years by dense overgrowth and benign neglect. Terri was still trying to get Lola to step outside and see for herself. All her previous ploys had failed.

"Lola, please? It's important. You won't actually be outside. The threshold is just here." Terri stood just inside the dining room doors. There was no getting Lola to budge from her throne. And God forbid all the drapes were open at the same time. The woman was like a vampire.

"I couldn't. I just couldn't," Lola May's southern accent got heavier when she was anxious.

"You can. Really you can," Terri urged. Lola giggled and shook her head no. Enough cajoling. Terri would petition on Lola's behalf anyway. She'd show Lola pictures.

"Yoohoo. Hellooo." *No.* Vanessa Vaughn arrived via the back lawn. Talk about an unhappy surprise. Both Lola and Terri looked around for somewhere to hide. Vanessa Vaughn walked into the dining room and announced, "I've already sent a petition on behalf of Lola May and myself to restore the gate with all due haste. Lola, here's your copy." Lola had not moved a muscle since Vanessa had entered the dining room. Lola was pretending to be invisible. Terri had seen her do this before. Vanessa scrutinized Lola closely and pronounced, "You're an old, old woman, Lola May. And nobody cares anymore what you look like. You ought to get out there and make the most of the time you have left." *Jesus, Vanessa way to sugarcoat it,* Terri thought.

"What's happening outside here?" Vanessa wanted to know with another "Hmm?" directed at Terri. Terri reluctantly followed Vanessa outside.

The grounds were shaping up. Herman had cut the remaining bramble away from the house and laid fresh sod around the cleaned and newly restored pool. Terri had touched up the nicked and chipped tiles with nail polish. The pool looked great, but she wasn't risking adding water until she had to, just in case Wonder Wear nail lacquer wasn't that wonderful.

The overgrown jungle still enveloped the bulk of the perimeter around Lola May's house. But now it contained a tunnel extending from the edge of the lawn to Herman's shed. It was four feet high and three feet wide. Vanessa peered down the tunnel then looked back at Terri expectantly with another, "Hmm?"

"Maybe it hurts his hump to hold a saw up high?" Terri offered.

"Herman needs more specific instructions, dear," Vanesa said, ever the authority. *Please go away. Shoo shoo,* Terri wished.

"Now about this week's luncheon. I was one of the Preservation Society's original founders, you know. They'll no doubt want to seat me at the head table, and you'll be seated with the other candidates for membership."

What wait? Nooo. Terri had forgotten she'd let herself get roped into a Palm Beach charity luncheon. Between Vanessa's imperiousness and Anthony and Angelo's expectations, there was no escaping. Bad enough she had to go to this tedious affair. Terri didn't want to hear chapter and verse about it now as well. *Wait. What? Preservation Society?*

"What? Yes? I mean, sure? But first, before that, Mrs. Vaughn, will you please come look at these?" Just because Vanessa was an insufferable windbag didn't mean she didn't know things. And she was a Preservation Society founder. Terri lead Vanessa to the recently exposed, golden columns flanking each of the dining room ocean side doors.

"These are—"

"I know what they are," Vanessa interrupted. "I'm on the board of several museums, you know." *Of course you are,* Terri thought. "And I can tell you these are museum quality columns."

"Thank you, Mrs. Vaughn. I thought they were valuable," Terri said.

"An understatement. You shouldn't allow them to rot out here in the elements, you know. By rights, they should be enclosed in the terraced room. That's what was originally here, after all."

Terri could have kissed her.

CHAPTER 12

THE BATH & RACQUET CLUB had warped, wood floors covered over with needlepoint carpets decorated with the club insignia. The insignia looked like a tennis racquet in a toilet bowl, if you asked Terri. It was an oval of yellow waves with a tennis racquet sticking out of it. *Who thought this was a good idea?* There were uncomfortable, aged wood benches and uncomfortable, faded floral sofas. There were acres of faded florally drapes at every window too, and the place smelled like mold. They kept the air conditioning at eighty and the drapes mostly shut.

What was with these oceanfront properties? Terri hadn't been in many, but wasn't the view what they paid for? It sure looked that way on the tax rolls. The dining room was a sea of hats and smelled like Bloomingdale's fragrance department. The Preservation Society luncheon guests were all seated on uncomfortable white, wood chairs around cloth-covered tables. Each table held an arrangement of pale, sparse flowers with a paper table number sticking out of its center.

"It looks like blind people made these arrangements," Vanessa remarked, peevishly. She hadn't been seated at the head table after all. Terri was seated beside her, thinking how handy Lola's invisible trick really was—if you could get the hang of it.

Some woman named Linda, Commissioner someone or other's wife, was droning on at the podium. She was so smug and delighted with herself Terri was glad Vanessa kept interrupting her. This time, Vanessa stood up to object and knocked her chair over.

"We can donate twice that amount by simply doing away with these frivolous luncheons where nobody eats a thing." *Here, here,* Terri thought, *and might I add the food's revolting?* Still Vanessa had a point. Vanessa continued, "Everyone here is too afraid they won't fit into their ball gowns for the evening event. Then they won't eat the elaborate dinner there either. It's a horrible, horrible waste." *Horrivle, horrivle.* "All while children in our own county go hungry." Vanessa was way up there on her high horse. At the podium, Mrs. Commissioner Linda forced a laugh into her voice.

"Vanessa dear, are you having zipper issues? Waiter, waiter. Don't serve her the profiteroles." This got a laugh from the luncheoners. Linda made a show of checking her watch and continued. "All excellent points, Vanessa, but if we don't move on we'll still be here for dinner. On a Tuesday, heaven forbid." *Jesus, could the food be worse at night?* Terri thought not.

There was more idiot giggling from the luncheoners and then Linda-Something-Commissioner's wife continued.

"Now it's time to discuss the Preservation Society Holiday House Dinner, our flagship event." For some reason, this had everyone bursting into a round of applause. "It's true, many charities have copied us. And imitation is the sincerest form of flattery. But I can say with complete confidence," Terri wondered if there was anything this woman couldn't say with complete confidence, "we are still the most coveted invitation on the island. So, in the tradition of remaining the very best, this year we are bestowing the great honor of hosting our event on Mrs. Ursula Lurie. Ursula, are you here? Is that you, dear, in the back?"

Seriously? Terri stood up to see. Ursula was, indeed, there, cowering behind her tablemates' giant brimmed hats at a table toward the back of the room. It was Terri's very own Ursula: the very nitwit who locked Terri outside on a thirty-second story balcony. First, Ursula and Ben Lurie had made her sign a redundant confidentiality agreement. All real estate dealings are confidential. Then Ursula detested everything Terri showed them. And then they locked her outside on a balcony to possibly die and were never heard from again.

Bastards.

"There you are, Ursula. Stand up. Up, up, up." She was instructed from the podium.

Yeah, stand up you inflatable, almost murderer, Terri silently cheered. Linda continued.

"Ursula has the most exquisite estate. It's the ideal setting for our Preservation Society Holiday House Dinner. Really marvelous. No expense was spared to make it perfect for our best event yet."

Ursula had managed a half-crouch, half-stand at her seat. She spoke at barely above a whisper. "That iz what I would like too. But the house iz not ready." Ursula was bright red with embarrassment and stammered badly in her heavy German accent. "Ze house. It is not ready. I am sorry for zis."

"Not ready? I've seen it." Linda barked into the microphone while the room vibrated with disapproval. This was apparently a terrible crime: not hosting the Preservation Society Holiday House Dinner.

Ursula's swollen lips almost quivered and tears threatened to dislodge her false eyelashes.

"My house cannot be for ze Preservation Society Holiday House Dinner. I apologize very much for zis," Ursula sniveled, whilst her tablemates stood on en masse and left her alone at the table. At the podium, Linda Commissioner's wife was relentless.

"This is astonishing. I can hardly believe, Ursula, you are reneging on hosting us. This puts us in a terrible bind." Terri wasn't an Ursula fan either, but who were these women, party-shaming her? Didn't they know charity began at home? Vanessa leaped into the breach.

"I will host the Preservation Society Holiday House Dinner. There. No bind at all."

That livened things right up. Speaker Linda Commissioner and her clones at the head table went berserk. Every slim, frosted blonde, pearl-wearing one of them had shrill objections. They were dead set against any Vanessa involvement. Terri understood this well. She tuned out their rancor and searched for something edible on the table. *Eureka.* She found a packet of cellophane-wrapped oyster crackers.

"Before we ask the candidates for new membership to stand, let's all give an enthusiastic round of applause to the Light House for the Blind, who made our beautiful centerpieces today."

Terri choked hard on her oyster crackers. Vanessa handed her an iced tea. It was terrible. Linda Commissioner continued at the podium.

"Now, if all those candidates for our Junior Committee would please stand at your seats." A half dozen twenty to thirty-somethings around the room stood at their tables. Vanessa whispered to Terri. "Stand up."

"I can't. Really," Terri was vibrating with laughter. And choking on the cracker.

"Don't be ridiculous. Go on, stand up." Vanessa reached over and gave Terri a hard little pinch. *What the hell?* It made Terri laugh harder.

******

Terri trailed behind Vanessa. She had gotten herself under control by the time the Preservation Society luncheon concluded and they were on their way to the valet. Terri thought she was home free, but no. Vanessa had spied a fat, barrel-chested old guy who looked like an extra in a period golf drama and veered off after him. He was wearing knickers with argyle sox and a beret with a blue and yellow pompom on top.

He and his companions, marginally less cartoonishly attired, were obviously trying to avoid them. Too bad for them. *And me*, Terri thought. Vanessa broke into a trot, calling out and dragging Terri along behind her.

"Judge. Judge, I must speak with you." The volume Vanessa could achieve whilst her teeth were firmly clenched was amazing. The judge and his companions stopped.

"Dear, this is Judge Beau Montgomery, Commissioner Scotty Berens, and Brinker Deeley. Gentlemen, this is Terri Somerville," Vanessa didn't stop for breath or how do-you-dos, which was fine by Terri. Terri assumed the Commissioner was Smug Linda, queen of the Preservation Society's, husband.

And she had met tubby Brinker Deeley the head flicker when he'd arrived out of the blue with a lowball offer for Lola May's house. Terri was happy not to be dragged into a chat with either of them. She was thinking about how good it would feel to change out of her luncheon clothes. And order a pizza. She was starving.

"Judge Montgomery, what has become of the petition for my gate?" Vanessa demanded.

Gate? This got Terri's full attention. An ungated path the length of Lola May's perimeter was almost as much of a drawback as the path itself. The judges's blue pompom bobbed as he laughed.

"Vanessa Vaughn. Look at you. Always a joy to see you."

"Bull donkey. I was assured my petition would receive swift attention. It's been a week. A week. You read it, didn't you?" Vanessa demanded.

"Yes, Vanessa. I read it. You've been obstructing access to government property with your gate. It seems clear to me. These laws are made for a reason."

Vanessa was incensed. "It's a turtle path, for God's sakes. Twice a year some kind of turtle ranger comes down our path wearing red coveralls and sticks tiny flags in my dune."

"Refresh me, Vanessa. That path's a running from the beach to the road, ain't it?" the judges good ol' boy routine escalated with his bullshit.

"You know exactly where it is." Vanessa said.

"Seems to me that makes it a national security issue, Vanessa. Now, that's not something a lil' county judge like me can decide."

"Bunk." Vanessa said, not mollified one bit. "You own this county." Vanessa accused. It was true. He'd inherited it from his father and his father before him. For generations, the Montgomery's flagrantly appointed their own relatives to the bench, county commissions, and town councils—nepotism be dammed. Combined, they were more powerful than any elected official and the first thing the Montgomerys did was amend the bylaws to keep it that way.

Vanessa told Terri all of this while driving Terri back to Lola May's estate, where Terri had left her car. After Vanessa accused the judge of owning the county he'd preened and laughed like Vanessa had paid him a compliment. Then he patted Vanessa's hand, winked at Terri, and walked off with the commissioner and Brinker Deeley, who had been waiting several feet away, like the lackies Terri suspected them of being.

The very next morning, Vanessa Vaughn was pounding stakes holding "Keep Out, Do Not Enter" signs into the ground at the head of the path. As usual, her dogs were with her: two big, old golden retrievers who dozed in the shade while Vanessa toiled. Suddenly, the dogs woke up and began barking.

Coming up the path from the beach were four surfers. Their sunbleached hair was wet and sandy and each had a surfboard tucked up under their arm. At dawn, they had paddled out to catch the Reef Road break two miles north and the current had washed them south. Their last wave had landed them behind Lola May's, and they were using the footpath as a cut through to the road. One of their girlfriends would be out driving Ocean Boulevard by now, scouting for them. Vanessa shouted the moment she saw them.

"Stop. You can't come through here. Go back. Stop." Seventy-five-year-old Vanessa, all 110 pounds of her, dressed in a pink and green floral shift dress with pearls and waving a hammer, wasn't much of a threat. The surfers had to go this way. The Bath & Racquet Club, their other alternative, always made a federal case over it and wasn't worth the extreme hassle. But cutting through the path wasn't a problem. The surfers had strategies.

Today's was the chicken game: both fun and effective. Clucking and laughing, they raced up the path directly at Vanessa, dodging around her at the last second. Vanessa shouted uselessly and shook her hammer. At the street, the surfers split up and took off in different directions, but Vanessa kept railing, "How dare you. Don't you come back here. I'll report you." Thwarted, Vanessa looked back down the path with dismay. There was further evidence of unwelcome foot traffic in the form of several empty beer cans and a ratty beach towel.

CHAPTER 13

TERRI MET MR. AND MRS. JASON Feb while waiting at Walgreens Drug Store to pick up her contact prescription. The Febs were seated beside her, studying a real estate magazine, looking pathetic and helpless. Terri broke her own rule of never speaking to strangers.

"Excuse me. You're holding that upside down." Now, five weeks and twenty-nine homes later, Terri was showing the Febs a very modest open-floor plan ranch house in a low-priced development. The Febs were twenty-something newlyweds who had met in a bible study group at their church, The Blessed Something Savior Our Lord—Terri couldn't remember the name of it. This was the Febs third look at this property. They wanted it, but had refused to make a written offer until the home passed a series of routine inspections.

The home inspector, Darryl Boyd, was (among other things) remarkably hairy. He had the kind of dark stubble at nine a.m. that made you think it probably extended all the way down his body. The back of his hands looked like puppies. He wore a yellow jumpsuit like a baggage handler or an exterminator and wandered from room to room with various tools and a clipboard. The electrical outlets, the washer and dryer, the lights, the air conditioning, the roof, the toilets, hot and cold running water, and a dozen more systems (from insulation to sewage) were to be examined for working condition.

While Darryl stuck forks in plugs, Jason Feb and his wife, who had only ever been introduced to Terri as Mrs. Feb, or referred to as "my wife," were reconsidering.

"We're a lot further away, and there's the car to consider. The Mrs. and me, we're praying for that car," Jason told Terri. He asked her: "When do we need to put money down?"

"As soon as I have all the signatures. Probably tomorrow. Will that be a problem?" Terri asked.

"No. No, I'm ready to make an offer. I just want to talk it over with Jesus first." *Jesus? Christ,* Terri thought. He was serious.

"Okay. Because you are eligible for more financing if you need it."

"No, no. The Lord will show me the way," Jason said.

"God. I mean, do you think he'll show you the way by say, 1:15? Because I'll need to cancel the rest of our appointments," Terri said.

Mrs. Feb, who until that moment never spoke a word, said, "You shouldn't ever refer to him that way. Our pastor says to say 'Jesus' or 'Our Lord' or else 'the Baby Jesus Christ our Savior.'"

"O—kay. Good to know. How about by 1:30?" Terri asked, then left the Febs to ponder the Baby Jesus Savior's schedule in the master bathroom while she went to answer her phone in the small dining room. It had fallen into a black hole inside her purse, under her briefcase, in her hugely oversized, canvas book bag. That thing held brochures, signs, rain boots, magazines, towels, hammers, art supplies, emergency Hostess snowballs (pink), and even surgical masks, which became a staple after Terri listed a former meth lab for sale. If Terri had two consecutive showings, she'd get a contact high. Now, she couldn't find her phone, which was ringing and ringing the Twilight Zone theme song. She didn't want the Febs to hear it and think she was some kind of pagan—or worse—a Scientologist. *Goddamnit, where is my phone? I mean, God Baby Savior Damnit.*

Terri found her phone. But everything else had slid off the table and dumped out onto the floor.

"Hello? I mean, hello. Terri here, Premium Property Partners Realty."

"Hello, Terri. It's Jud. How's it going?" Jud was Terri's seller, and she liked him a lot. He was a long-distance trucker who had married his high school sweetheart, Lucy. They were jumbo people, an easy five hundred pounds combined, with four children the size of bears. Jud was devastated when his mother died recently, but it meant he'd inherited her home, which was three times as big as this one. They couldn't wait to move in but needed to sell this house first. For every reason, Jud and his family could hardly wait.

"Well," Terri whispered into her phone so the Febs wouldn't overhear. "They're here with me now. I'm certain they're going to make you a written offer today. Darryl, he's the home inspector, is here too. He's moving along quickly. Always a good sign because it means he hasn't found any problems. He said everything looked in good order, and he was almost finished. Hello? Hello? You're breaking up? Hello? Jud, you're breaking up." Terri couldn't hear Jud. All she heard was crackling, some silence, and something about the stove. "I really can't hear you. What about the stove?"

In the kitchen behind Terri there was a big red flash, a *WHOOSH*, and a *SCREAM*. Then many things happened at once. The fire alarm went off—screeching in their ears. Terri dropped her cell phone and flung open the swinging door dividing the dining room from the kitchen. Darryl, the inspector, stood at the sink, beating out his flaming clipboard. The Febs crowded in behind Terri, holding hands and praying.

Terri saw all the hair on the left side of Darryl's head and face was singed off: hair stubble, eyebrow, all of it. His hand looked like it had been waxed. White ash snowed down on him until he gave up beating out the flames and drowned his clipboard in the sink.

Terri said, "The fire alarm works."

This was ignored.

"Goddamnit." Darryl shouted among a dozen other profanities. His jumpsuit was charred. The Febs prayed.

"Are you okay?"

"Do I fucking look okay?" he snapped. Darryl didn't look that injured to Terri. While the denuding was extreme, Terri could argue it was an improvement. Likewise, the house, apart from the mess in the sink and the back left burner on the stove, looked okay. Terri opened all the windows and doors. The fire alarm thankfully stopped screaming. Darryl was still enraged and stomped to the bathroom to look in the mirror. Terri followed.

"Holy shit. Holy shit. That's it. I'm fucking out of here," Darryl said.

"No, please. You were almost done. Everything else worked fine," Terri pleaded while Darryl examined himself and his shiny, new left side.

Shit.

He was probably a Republican too.

"You couldn't pay me to pass inspection on this house. And I get paid plenty to pass all kinds of pieces of shit." Failing a home inspection was a sure way to kill a house sale.

"But it's not a piece of shit. You—" Terri dashed back to the dining room and found a blank home inspection form from among the contents of her fallen book bag. She returned triumphantly to the bathroom and gave it to Darryl. He gave himself a last disgusted look in the mirror and took the form from Terri. He reached for his pen in the breast pocket of his shirt, but it had melted into a "u" shape: Darryl's final indignity.

"That is it." he shouted and marched into the dining room, where he nabbed a pen from among Terri's spilled belongings on the floor. "Here we go. Here we are. Stove—FAIL."

"I'll say," Terri agreed, hovering. "I'm very sorry."

"Roof—fail. Septic—fail. Water heater—fail. Electrical—fail." Darryl made furious Xs beside each system.

"You can't do that." Terri protested.

"Watch me," Darryl said. "Insulation—fail."

Terri was not having this. Jud deserved more space, and if Terri spent any more time with the Febs, she'd become an atheist. "You told me yourself the gas was always the last thing you inspected. And you said everything else seemed to be in good shape."

"Unlike myself." Darryl snarled, catching another glance at himself in the dining room mirror.

"Fine," Terri said. "I'll pay you to write up the honest, passing inspection report this house earned," Terri told him.

"You don't got that kind of money. Every other developer with their shoddy, paper wiring and Chinese drywall slips me 10 bills just to say hello," Darryl growled. Terri reached over and snatched the report right out of Darryl's hand. He was shocked. Then he tried to grab it back.

"Hey, gimme that—"

"No," Terri said. And they did the "keep away" thing around the small dining room table. Neither of the Febs had said a word since the kitchen combusted, despite things getting ever more physical. Terri faked right, then left, then tripped herself on a chair leg. CRASH. The Febs TSKED at her, like Terri had deliberately flung herself onto the dining room floor. But Darryl was jolted back into rational behavior by Terri's fall. With another curse, he reached out his hand to help her up and noticed Terri's sketch pad lying open on the floor.

"What's this?" Darryl asked.

"This here?" Terri picked up the sketch. It was a watercolor of the house they were standing in, featuring Jud's obese beagle (named Michelin) lying on the lawn in front.

"This is the 'congratulations your house sold' present that I don't need anymore, thanks to you." Darryl considered this information. The Febs inched closer to the action, riveted.

"Can you paint a ferret?" Darryl asked.

Huh?

"A small beast, ferret?" Terri clarified.

"Yeah," Darryl said. "He's pretty small. For a ferret." *Ah.* Terri understood. She'd just bought herself an inspection report.

CHAPTER 14

TERRI USED HER own set of keys to open Lola May's front door. "Hi, Lola. How's it going?" she called out. Terri was toting a box of paints and dragging a tarp with her. It was 10:30 p.m. Lola was parading back and forth down the front hall in an Amelia Earhart-style flying uniform with shiny, knee-high black boots and trailing a white satin scarf. One side of the hall was lined with side-by-side arched, stained glass windows. They had been boarded over for a hurricane in 1978 and hadn't seen the light of day since. Terri discovered them behind more thorny bushes and, armed with Ben and Jerry's, she'd convinced Herman to trim it all back and pry the inch thick plywood off the windows. Not a small or easy task, but Herman accomplished it to make Terri happy. He was becoming quite smitten with her.

The hall across from the windows was lined with mirrors which, sing Hosannas, made the hall look twice as large as it actually was.

Maybe, just maybe, all this effort would pay off, Terri thought. And she could get Lola a great price for her home. One Lola could actually live happily on afterward. And, of course, there was the killer commission Terri stood to make. She hadn't even let herself consider the second commission she could earn, buying Lola May's next residence. No. She wouldn't count that ninety-five-year old chicken until it hatched.

Lola was stopping before each mirror as she made her way down the hall. "It's awfully difficult to look terrified and bursting with glee all at once," Lola declared and made a face at herself in the mirror. "Yet, you do it so easily. Here I've been practicing all the live long night," Lola drawled. Terri thought Lola looked like she had gas. "But I shall persevere, sweetie. Don't you worry," Lola told Terri.

"I won't," Terri said and set about laying down her tarp and lining up various pots of paints. She'd been working at odd hours faux painting those areas of the house that had devolved from charming antique to rotted crap. Tonight, Terri was working on the Moroccan tile stair risers that were nearly worn away of all pattern. She'd been putting it off because it was a huge pill to do. The stairs were narrow, steep, and spiral, and she had to work from a ladder for most of it, hunched over, twisted and off balance. Not at all the ideal place to be when the screaming started.

****

Muffy Deeley was having the worst school break ever.

Her parents, Beth and Brinker Deeley, had moved them from Palm Beach into a West Palm Beach condominium, and now her Palm Beach friends were blowing her off. Muffy used to live at Dee Lee, a ramshackle colonial house situated on the north end of Palm Beach Island, where the homes are so precious they name them. Dee Lee belonged to Great Grammy Deeley, even though living there was a nightmare because Grammy lived there with them, it was way too small with only two bathrooms and it had no air conditioning. But at least living there, everyone knew how important Muffy was: that her family was old Palm Beach. That she had superior breeding. But then Grammy up and died and Muffy's parents sold the house.

"How could you do this? Are you both stupid?" Muffy raged at her parents when they told her of the move.

"It's only for a year, Muffy. If you don't like it, don't come home," her mother Beth told her with her mother's trademark warmth. Muffy should have listened to her mother. Her important friends were treating her like some West Palm townie, and none of them had shown up tonight, even though they all said they would.

Only Stamford and Porky showed, as usual, and tripped over themselves dancing attendance on her. And who wanted either of them? Sure, Stamford's parents were rich, but they didn't even belong to the Everglades Club. And Porky wasn't good looking enough for Muffy, although he did dress well. How pathetic that Thirsty Thursdays at the Bath & Racquet Club had become the highlight of Muffy's trip home.

To jolly Muffy out of her snit, Porky and Stamford stole a pitcher of screwdrivers and a quart of vodka off the bar. They fortified themselves, then ditched Thirsty Thursday and headed out to hunt for the monster again, dragging Muffy along with them. Monster rumors had been circulating at the Bath & Racquet Club for as long as anyone could remember. The rumors would bubble up and die down again with each generation. Muffy thought the stories were complete horseshit: something parents told to get their kids to behave. The monster was not real. But Porky and Stamford were determined to prove Muffy wrong.

The last time they had drunk enough liquid courage to go monster hunting, some imbecile smashed into crazy Mrs. May's gate. The jerk killed himself and totally ruined their plans. Muffy wouldn't have gone with them this time except it was their last night to do anything because everyone had to go back to boarding school in the morning.

The three of them moved furtively along the Bath & Racquet Club's front hedgerow, which ran alongside the road. The party back at the Bath & Racquet Club grew fainter with each unsteady step.

"I overheard Commissioner Berens and the judge talking about him. He's real. I swear to God." Porky slurred, loudly. Muffy and Stamford shushed him, then fell over themselves laughing. The screwdrivers had kicked in.

"Hey, this isn't some bullshit story made up to scare little kids. Remember Edward Delft? He was in, like, eighth grade when we were in kindergarten? His older brother. The monster fucking ate his eye out. Just ate it out. Like it was an olive," Porky said.

"So?" said Muffy, ever unimpressible. "It's not like anyone died."

"Yeah? Well, what about all those kids who turned up missing?" Porky argued.

"What kids who turned up missing? Like one kid in a hundred years has gone missing in Palm Beach," Muffy scoffed.

"Okay, that kid. That one kid. The monster ate him," Porky said.

"Then he's a hundred-year-old monster, and he's already dead." Muffy had an answer for everything.

"Guys, check it out. No gate. We can just walk right in, easy-peasy," Stamford said.

They'd walked the width of Lola May's property and arrived at the head of the path between Lola May's and Vanessa Vaughn's. As Stamford pointed out, there was nothing to prevent them from waltzing right in. No yellow tape, no gate, no nothing.

"There's no monster living in the woods here. No way. You're just trying to scare me into flipping out or something so you can Instagram it. That's a really shitty thing to do," Muffy accused the boys and hiccupped. Stamford lit a joint and walked down the path with Porky.

It was dark and moonless. He turned around and taunted Muffy, who had lagged behind.

"Better catch up. The monsters's fast. He'll getcha before we can save you."

"You. Are. Full. Of. Shit." Muffy said, but caught up with the boys quickly enough. She traded a hit off Stamford's joint for her bottle of vodka and then took her vodka back. Stamford passed the joint to Porky.

"Ow. Don't drop it." Stamford said.

It was really dark out. They could barely make out each other's faces. Porky foraged off the path for a bit into Lola May's jungle, and Muffy and Stamford followed. Porky turned around after capturing a long stick. He waded forward and wielded it, sword like.

"Here, monster, monster, monster." Porky whispered, loudly. "Here, monster, monster."

"Wait," Stamford said. "We gotta like sneak up on him." Stamford HUMMED the Jaws theme song and, with this fanfare, he whipped a wicked looking hunting knife out of his pocket. It gleamed evilly in the darkness. Muffy's perverted little heart fluttered.

"Shhh," Porky shushed and got suddenly serious. "Shut up. I think I see something."

They shuffled forward. Muffy and Stamford were still snickering. Then, like Terri had done weeks before, Muffy walked right into the side of Herman's shed before she saw it. "OOOPH."

"Holy shit. What the fuck is this?" Stamford whispered.

"I don't know," Porky answered stupidly, and they all started laughing again. Stamford flicked his cigarette lighter. It took him about forty flicks to achieve a flame because he was really stoned.

"AAAHHHH." they all screamed at once.

"AAARAAAAAAAAAAAAAAAH." There was Herman, crouched

against his hut and stiller than stone. They were less than a foot away from him.

****

Terri nearly fell off the ladder when she heard the screams. She managed to not upset the little paint pots balanced up there with her on the way down. Mrs. Irish hustled in from the kitchen, and she and Terri both ran to the dining room, where the outside doors stood open. Lola was sitting contentedly on her throne, admiring the prisms in the chandelier.

"Oh, Lola, for a minute I thought. God, phew. Did you hear that?" Terri asked her.

"I'm not deaf, sweetie. Just some kids playing. They're always playing." *Playing what? Self-immolation?*

"I think I'll go check it out," Terri said and swiped the poker from the dining room fireplace, just in case, before she slipped out the door.

Two more tunnels had been pruned through Lola May's jungle to the outer reaches of the property. *Please God, don't let there be snakes,* Terri thought and steeled herself. She took the tunnel leading back toward Herman's shed. Terri thought the screams had come from there. She swept her poker low in front of her and moved slowly, like you move when you don't want to get where you're going. And you can't see anything. Terri heard rustling noises ahead of her and stopped.

"Herman? Hey, Herm? Are you out here?" Terri whispered loudly, took a step, and nearly collided with Vanessa Vaughn in the darkness.

"Watch where you're going, dear." Vanessa snapped. She was wearing a bathrobe and carrying a rifle.

O—kay. Terri decided to stick with Vanessa and not become an accidental shooting victim. Terri followed her. They walked to the beach end of the path and then backtracked until they were roughly parallel with Herman's shed.

"Herman? Herman, where are you?" Vanessa called out. They listened and heard nothing. Terri pulled her phone from her pocket and pushed flashlight mode. They crept around Herman's shed and found him lying on his side in the fetal position. His hands covered his face, and they were both covered in blood.

****

Terri didn't remember calling 911. She remembered flinging herself to her knees beside Herman and crying most unhelpfully until Mrs. Vaughn took her phone away and gave the 911 operator their address. Within minutes, a tiny triage had been set up in Vanessa Vaughn's beautiful, circular driveway, consisting of one police car and one ambulance. Herman and Terri sat side by side on the ambulance's open tailgate while a medic knelt behind them and stitched up the cut on Herman's head. Terri was holding Herman's hand, and she was nearly as bloody as he was.

"You are going to keep hold of his hands, right? 'Cause if you're not, someone else is, or I'm not doing this," the medic said, as if Herman couldn't hear him. Terri wanted to slap the guy. Hadn't he ever seen a walleyed hunchback before? *Who'd he think Quasi Modo was?* But she said nothing because she wanted him to be gentle with Herman. And fast.

Vanessa brought out stale biscuits and worse coffee and determinedly foisted it on everyone there. Even Herman wouldn't eat the biscuits. A policewoman, to her future regret, asked Vanessa Vaughn for a statement. Terri tuned out everything but the highlights.

"It's happened before. It's not some hoodlums from West Palm Beach either. It's rich, privileged hoodlums from the Bath & Racquet Club next door to Lola May's. Their parents are to blame, you know. Never giving them a good thrashing when they should have," Vanessa said.

The policewoman asked, "Can Herman describe his assailants?"

"Given an eternity. You've met him," Vanessa said with her usual derision through her tightly closed teeth. Had Herman been given that eternity and opportunity, he would have corroborated Vanessa's speculations. Adding that the handsome one, who incidentally didn't know how to work a knife, pissed himself. The fat one ran away crying. And the girl smashed Herman over the head with a vodka bottle while screaming invectives at her friends. Vanessa continued now that she had the policewoman trapped.

"I know it was those heathen club children. Hmm? You ought to have a biscuit. Take one, go on."

Herman was unconsciously crushing Terri's hand.

"Herman. Herm. Ease up, you're crushing my hand," Terri said, adding, "Can you hurry it up?" to the medic.

It was past one in the morning when the ambulance left. Terri was jet-lag tired. Crying tired.

"Mrs. Vaughn? I've got to go home."

"You'll go when we're done. Hmm?" Vanessa said, still carrying the rifle. She was still carrying her rifle. *Guess I'll go when we're done,* Terri thought. She trailed Vanessa down her driveway toward the road and winced when the *ERRR-CHINK* sound confirmed that Vanessa had closed her driveway gates with a remote control. She finally put the rifle down, only to pick up a hefty flashlight. Vanessa searched the ground around her until she spotted a large yellow plastic container. She picked it up and thrust it into Terri's arms. *No.*

"Follow me," Vanessa said and tramped across her perfectly landscaped lawn to the head of the dreaded path between her property and Lola May's. There were no cars on Ocean Boulevard that late at night and all signs of the crash had been cleared away. The only things left were the two iron lion head posts the gate used to span.

An hour later, Terri was still there. Standing. She and Vanessa had dumped out all the yellow container's contents, and Terri was holding the flashlight while Vanessa worked. Vanessa was attaching a mechanism to one of the lion head posts where the gate used to be attached.

Vanessa was as invigorated by this task, as Terri was nodding off where she stood. "I've done it. I've got this thing with the prong lined up with the cone thing with wires. The two bits connected with a very satisfying click. Hmm?" Vanessa declared, snapping Terri out of her stupor.

"Huh, what?"

"I've done it. Now, what does it say next dear?" Terri was helping Vanessa install an electronic fencing device across the head of the path. Terri read the teeny-weeny printed directions that she'd crumpled inadvertently.

"It says—Mrs. Vaughn, it says it's for *cattle*."

CHAPTER 15

TERRI HAD SPENT the whole afternoon in her Premium Property Partners office cubicle researching regulations on Palm Beach County's historic landmarks. *Kill me,* she thought. There were thirty-two hundred designated historic landmarks in Palm Beach County. They included an amazing assortment of buildings. Many were much younger than fifty years old and hundreds looked derelict. Yet, they were all designated historic landmarks.

Vanessa Vaughn was right about Lola May's columns though. Those were very valuable. But it was anyone's guess as to whether or not they could be removed and sold. Terri could make the argument they had to be moved or they'd eventually erode completely. She could also make a better argument that the whole terraced room should be restored to protect the columns where they stood.

Premium Property Partner's attorney told Terri to get approval from whomever governed historic landmarks for whatever she decided to do, and it had turned into a huge chore. Terri found all kinds of conflicting criteria for receiving a historic landmark designation. More aggravating was she couldn't figure out which of the many historic societies, clubs, and organizations in Palm Beach County had the final legal authority. It was driving her mad.

She'd been at it for hours.

Joel kept popping in and out. In and out. He was ticking down the time she had left until her date. Joel was fixing Terri up with his stepbrother that night, and they were all going out to dinner in Fort Lauderdale to a restaurant renowned for its key lime pie. Joel wanted Terri to brush her hair and put on some lipstick and change into something more flattering.

"This isn't flattering?" Terri asked, sincerely.

"Did you dress in the dark? In someone else's clothes?" Joel said. Her skirt was too big and hung askew and her sleeves were rolled up to two different lengths. She was oblivious. The fifth and last pop in Joel continued to stand in the doorway, tapping his foot, until Terri hit print. She wasn't done. *Drat.* She'd make Joel read what research she had out loud to her on their way to dinner: a nerve wracking forty-five minute drive down I-95.

Despite Terri driving like a maniac to make up for lost time, they arrived a few minutes late to meet Joel's stepbrother, Robert. As Joel expected, Robert was a dick about it. Joel and he had always had a chilly relationship but Terri's last few dates were so appalling Joel figured even Robert would be a step up. Robert was at least a reasonably stable, good-looking, fully employed American Airlines pilot— a quantum leap up from Terri's last date with a bipolar tattoo artist who came to pick Terri up in a forty-foot RV camper with his mother inside. Yes, he deserved points for being up front about his life and personal issues, but he did not deserve to drive them to a date with Terri. Despite her dressing like a refugee and never brushing her hair unless repeatedly reminded, Terri was a beauty. And smart and funny. And Robert was the only straight bachelor Joel knew.

The waiter served Terri a slice of key lime pie and said, "I'm terribly sorry. This is the last piece of key lime pie. The kitchen has run out."

"That's okay," Terri said. "We'll split it up." and she began carving it into three slivers.

"Don't be stupid. There's not enough there to even bother," Robert said.

"That's what's special about it," Terri told him. "This is all that's left in the world. It's like gold." Joel tasted a tiny morsel from his allotted sliver.

"Superb," Joel declared. "A perfect ending. If there were more, we'd only snarf it up piggishly."

"Yeah, that makes sense." Robert devolved to his full, charmless self. "I'm so glad we came all the way here for their famous key lime pie, which they don't even have and now you're saying you don't even want."

"Come on, Robert, lighten up," Joel said.

"Hey Joel, I didn't ask for this little fix-up," Robert snapped back.

"Robert, what's wrong with you? Terri is a doll. She's not only gorgeous. She happens to be the sweetest, coolest—" Joel's glowing assessment was interrupted by two uniformed policemen appearing on either side of Terri's chair, flashing their badges.

"Are you Terri Somerville, 1543 Decatur Avenue, West Palm Beach, Florida?" one of the policemen asked.

"Yes?" Terri did her nervous question thing.

"Ma'am, you're under arrest. You have the right to remain silent." And they lifted Terri up out of her chair while mirandizing her.

"Criminal?" Robert shouted at Joel. "She's the sweetest, coolest criminal you've ever met? Thanks, Joel. I'm so glad you thought to fix her up with me."

The uniformed cops put Terri in handcuffs and hauled her out of the restaurant, one on each side. The restaurant was silent, riveted.

Their heads swiveled back and forth between Terri and the cops and "The Joel vs. Robert Drama" back at the table. There was a lot happening simultaneously.

"And you can pay for dinner too." Robert spat, then flung his napkin at Joel and stormed out as his closing salvo.

CHAPTER 16

TERRI WAS SITTING alone in an interrogation room inside the West Palm Beach Police Station when Detective E. Shay walked in. He was frowning at her hard. Terri was just relieved he'd shown up at all and gave him a dazzling smile in return.

Damnit. E. Shay did not want to be irresistibly attracted to this probable mental case.

"I didn't know who else to call," Terri explained by way of a greeting.

"Terri, I'm a detective, not a lawyer," E. Shay said.

"But you work here. And you are here," Terri pointed out irrefutably. E. Shay knew he was losing this war.

"Did they tell you what you're being charged with?" E. Shay asked her.

"I—I electrocuted someone?"

"Jesus Christ. Who? Are they dead?" *Of course you electrocuted someone. I never fall for a woman unless she's deranged. I need deep, deep therapy.* E. Shay was pulled back from this reverie by a knock, followed by the interrogation room door opening.

"Do you have a lawyer?" E. Shay asked.

"No? I can't afford a lawyer," Terri said. E. Shay continued to frown really hard at her.

Walk away, E. Shay. Walk away while you still can, he repeated like a mantra, but all he said out loud was, "Then don't say anything. Seriously. Zip it."

The group arriving from down the hall included Vanessa Vaughn. She was escorted by two irritated officers. This evening Vanessa's ensemble included a brocade evening gown with handcuffs, earning the arresting officers a sharp scowl from E. Shay.

"Bracelets? Really?" E. Shay asked, referring to the handcuffs on a woman of seventy-five.

"She told her dogs to kill us," one of the officers said.

"The dog's name is Killam. I kept telling you that. Killam and Sheila, named after my mother's Irish butler and his wife," Vanessa said.

Terri and E. Shay instinctively shared a look. God help him, if Terri burst out laughing, E. Shay would too. This was bad. Vanessa spied Terri.

"There you are, Terri. Don't cower. There's a thread hanging from your skirt."

Terri skootched herself further behind E. Shay, keeping the officers between herself and Vanessa.

"I'll handle this." Vanessa took command. "We're well within our legal rights, you know. I am prepared to explain in full detail how this is a travesty of justice."

"Not to me, hallelujah," said one of the cops, and he and his partner beat it, leaving E. Shay alone in the small room with Vanessa Vaughn and Terri.

"What in this world are we doing here at all? I demand we be moved to Palm Beach," Vanessa said. She continued to question and endlessly demand until Vanessa's lawyer arrived a half hour later.

E. Shay had a short, private chat with him and summonsed a woman patrol officer. She was directed to deliver Terri and Vanessa to the Palm Beach Town Courthouse, where a special arraignment had been arranged by Mrs. Vaughn's council, who would meet them there.

They soon arrived at Palm Beach's courthouse. It was a beautiful, landmark building that looked like Ralph Lauren had art directed it himself. Outside and inside were equally impressive. It reeked of old establishment money. The lobby was a small, exquisite rotunda, and the courtroom was furnished in elegant burlwood and dulled bronze. Even Judge Montgomery looked resplendent, costumed in his robes and seated upon the dais. He was right out of central casting, with his jowls hanging over his collar and his tuxedo cuffs peeking out from beneath his robe's sleeves. The judge had apparently been attending the same event Vanessa was dressed for. He was attended by two uniformed officers and a court reporter.

At the defendant's table, Terri sat beside Vanessa Vaughn, and Vanessa sat between Terri and Vanessa's beleaguered attorney, Eric Greenfield. *Poor guy,* was all Terri could think. Eric was a young, earnest, nervous type with damp hands and an unfortunate, Ichabod Crane body type, Adam's apple included. He was the perfect junior partner to sic Vanessa on. Terri was sure his senior law partners were hazing him. She was also sure he was a really, really good attorney. He'd gotten them a hearing here at ten o'clock at night. Amazing.

****

E. Shay worked at his desk at the West Palm Beach Police Station for eleven whole minutes and thirty-eight seconds after Terri and Mrs. Vaughn left before he couldn't take it anymore. He stood up and practically ran to his car thinking, *Don't go there; do not go there, you moron,* the whole way. He slipped quietly into the last row of the gallery. Except for an old, white-haired janitor who mopped between pews, E. Shay was the only spectator. Judge Montgomery banged his gavel.

"I hereby sentence you both to forty hours of community service."

Vanessa opened her mouth to object for the six thousandth time, but Eric Greenfield was faster.

"Thank you, Your Honor."

Then Greenfield spoke pleadingly to Vanessa, "It's reasonable. Please, Mrs. Vaughn. You already do more volunteering in any given week then this penalty requires. They didn't fingerprint you. You haven't been put through a formal intake. After your forty hours community service is complete, your record will be expunged. Please, Mrs. Vaughn, this is good." Vanessa kept them in suspense for a full minute, then conceded with an imperious nod. Terri and Eric Greenfield, Esquire, and E. Shay all breathed a huge sigh of relief. Then Judge Montgomery continued, "Your community service will be conducted at the Everglades Rehabilitation and Detention Center." Montgomery pounded his gavel once.

Vanessa leapt up. "Everglades? I protest." She had surprising volume.

"Mrs. Vaughn, please," Greenfield stood up beside her.

"Vanessa, you've electrocuted a man." Judge Montgomery roared from the bench. All his previous laconic, good ol' boy shtick was gone.

"He's a vagrant. And he's fine now." Vanessa shouted back in her lockjaw shout.

"He sustained third-degree burns." the judge barked. They were arguing like children.

"Through Myrna Allcot's stolen sable coat. That heathen was out burgling my neighborhood. He stole Myrna's coat. And her stunning collection of Flemish silver before he trespassed on our path and shocked himself. We should be receiving commendations of merit for capturing him," Vanessa declared.

"Dear God, woman, without that coat the man would be dead." Judge Montgomery pointed out.

"And that's a bad thing?"

****

Terri stood alone in front of the Palm Beach Town Courthouse. E. Shay pulled up beside her and rolled down his window.

"Need a lift?" he asked.

Be cool, Terri told herself and jumped in his car with unbridled enthusiasm. She was energized with excitement and smiling from ear to ear. She couldn't help it. She totally had a crush on this E. Shay detective.

He always looked at her with an intense ghost-smile that was so appealing, like he was smiling at her against his will.

It *was* against his will. E. Shay was very happy too. Too happy. Terri shouldn't make him this happy. He didn't even know her. Just that she was probably bats. *Damn.* He had it bad. E. Shay told himself to shake it off. Then thought, *Screw it. Dive right in.* The more he knew, the less he was bound to like.

He said, "Want to tell me your life story?"

"Want to fall asleep at the wheel and kill us?"

E. Shay bit his lip, trying not to laugh. *Shit.* She cracked him up too. "That dull?" He asked.

"Yes." Terri admitted with enthusiasm.

"Come on. What about Herman?"

"Oh. Well, recently things have been livelier. But you know all about that." E. Shay had heard everything in the courthouse. Terri had seen him sneak in right after Judge Montgomery arrived. They'd parted company back at the West Palm P.D. when he'd turned her and Vanessa over to the uniformed woman officer.

"Couldn't we talk about something else?" Terri asked.

"Such as?"

"Such as, are you married?" Terri asked him. Shay burst out laughing.

"No. Got any more questions?"

"No? Yes? Want to know my address?"

"I know your address. Remember?"

"Yes?" *Yes? Nitwit. Think of something clever to say.* Terri silently scolded herself.

They drove on in silence. Terri fiddled with an electronic cuff lying on the seat between them. She correctly assumed it was some kind of house arrest ankle bracelet. It had a battery hatch and a serial number and was stamped with Everglades Rehabilitation and Detention Center, where she and Vanessa would serve their forty community service hours. It looked awful to Terri.

This doesn't bode well, she thought and must have made a horrible face because E. Shay started laughing again and said, "You'll be fine. Forty hours is nothing."

But then again, the Rehabilitation and Detention Center was harsh duty. E. Shay got a bad smell from the place right from the start. The center was built as an interim holding pen for both indicted and convicted prisoner overflow from all Palm Beach County law enforcement services combined: a bad plan. It meant Palm Beach County Sheriff's prisoners—prostitutes and drunk drivers—were all thrown in the same holding cells with the FBI's gang prisoners and Homeland Security's prisoners. It was also a transfer center between jail and court, court and sentencing, and sentencing and prison. With the constant turnover and ordinary interagency confusion, prisoners, paperwork and evidence regularly went missing.

It was an open joke in the Palm Beach County's Sheriff's Department. If you had a reluctant suspect you wanted to come to their senses or a prisoner you wanted to simply lose, the Everglades Rehab and Detention Center was the way to go. E. Shay worked out of the office there as seldom as possible. This wasn't going to be a pleasant experience for Terri. He hoped it would scare her enough to kept her out of trouble in the future.

E. Shay stopped his car in front of Terri's building, put the car in park, but kept the motor running.

"Terri, I don't want to see you in the police station ever again," he said.

"Okay. What about the library? Or the post office? A non-penal municipal building?"

"I mean it, Terri. You'll end up in real trouble."

"I know. I'm sorry." Terri hopped out of the car, then leaned back in. "Do you want to come up?" E. Shay chuckled. "And see my drawings?" Terri added.

E. Shay burst out laughing. He couldn't help himself. Terri burst out laughing too. She continued, "You can tell me the truth. I'm un-insultable."

"Apparently," Shay said, looking at her standing there. She looked so frigging beautiful. Also, like maybe she'd been assaulted, but E. Shay was used to that already. Oh God, he was already used to her. And even that made him want her more, not less. He had to get the ef out of there. Fast. "It's late. And I'm on duty," E. Shay said and drove away without waiting for her to get safely inside.

Terri stood at the curb, baffled.

CHAPTER 17

THE EVERGLADES REHABILITATION and Detention Center was an enormous, concrete building without windows. It was located eighty-eight miles as the crow flies from Palm Beach Island. It was at the very edge of the county line in the middle of a swampy scrub surrounded by barbed wire fencing. The last thirty minutes of the drive were like driving through a terrarium. There were low, swampy bushes and high-tangled trees dripping vines Terri knew were filled with snakes. She hated snakes. The unrelenting vegetation dripped on both sides of the road. This was very much like Lola May's property on steroids, and Terri began to understand Vanessa's fierce objections to coming out to this Godforsaken place. She didn't want to get out of the car.

Terri was dressed as usual, like she'd been airlifted from some natural disaster and Sister Mary Margaret had taken mercy on her at the convent and loaned her clothes to see her home because she'd lost all. Which turned out wasn't a bad look for the Rehabilitation and Detention Center. Vanessa wore a peach Chanel suit with a little veiled hat and pearls.

She was wearing pearls.

"You can't expect us to counsel these—these people," Vanessa imperiously informed Belle in her most superiorly toned lockjaw. Belle was the director of the mandatory service program. She was an incredibly fit, older woman and a thirty-year veteran of the detention center. Belle was literally counting the days until her retirement and not inclined to make allowances for anyone, least of all Vanessa Vaughn in her pearls. Belle had shown Terri and Vanessa to a large, drab classroom with instructions to assist the prisoners in understanding their post-prison options. There were stacks of brochures laid out on a table that was bolted to the floor at the head of the classroom. Some were for trade schools or getting a GED. Others were maps marked with bus routes, soup kitchens, and rehab centers. Bibles were stacked against one wall.

"We're here to do community service. We're not professional social workers. As you can see, we aren't the least qualified for this," Vanessa objected again. The prisoners had begun to assemble in the classroom, and Vanessa became more adamant with each new arrival. Terri couldn't blame her. They were a scary looking group. Terri expected gang warfare to break out at any moment.

"Fine. You can collect their urine samples and bring them to the lab," Belle said. That shut Vanessa up.

"Wait." Terri cried. "I watched a lot of Oprah in high school. I can do this." Belle pointed to the stack of pamphlets on the table and left without another word.

Vanessa picked up a pamphlet in a sulk and sat down behind the large table that served as a desk, leaving Terri standing alone and facing a sea of surly, dangerous looking prisoners in their classroom. They were haphazardly seated on benches that were bolted to the floor. Many were impossible to distinguish either by age, race, or gender. The room had one door with a small window with grimy frosted glass. Terri could see two big guards with rifles standing just outside. *Why don't they stand just inside?* she thought.

Also, Vanessa was too small to hide behind.

"God," Terri inadvertently groaned out loud. Instantly there were protests from the prisoners. *Shit. Now they think I'm some holy roller preaching fire and brimstone and go, Jesus, go.* "I'm sorry, I'm sorry." Terri quickly apologized. "I didn't mean God. I swear there's no God here. I mean, never mind. I'm sorry?" The room had gotten quiet and all eyes were on Terri. She still stood because Vanessa took the only chair behind the table. Vanessa was sitting on it, tapping her foot at Terri expectantly. Terri picked up a pamphlet and read aloud.

"Careers in refrigeration and air conditioning repair." This started a small profane chorus of multilingual shouts as to how hot Terri was. Terri chose another brochure. "Earn your GED by mail." Again the sentiment in the room was expressed. "Die, bitch." Still, Terri persevered through more than a dozen pamphlets for vocational schools, rehab programs, support groups, and free clinics all to a resounding, "Go fuck yourself," from the increasingly hostile looking detainees. Vanessa sat there in a silent tiff, barely looking up.

"Well, Oprah, you've successfully incited these heathens even more. Now what will you do, hmm?" You could have heard a pin drop at Vanessa's words. The prisoners looked so incredulous Terri almost started laughing, but as soon as they'd translated Vanessa lockjaw into gang speak they got even madder.

"Whoa. No, Mrs. Vaughn, they're not heathens. They're—" Terri snatched up a random pamphlet and read aloud, "they're 'the future nail extension technicians of America', by God. Shit, excuse the God reference," Terri added.

"What's wrong with God?" Vanessa barked all clenching teeth.

Shit, Vanessa have you no sense of self-preservation? Terri thought, looking at their audience. *These criminals who are tattooed and pierced, skin-headed, and probably gang members, drug addicted, homeless, and maybe mental patients all hate us. No—you.* Terri amended in her mind. *They hate you.*

"Look at them," Vanessa said. "They're deliberately trying to frighten us."

"And succeeding," Terri pointed out.

"I didn't say they didn't do it well," Vanessa conceded. "Dear, scaring people is hardly a career path." Vanessa said.

"I know. It's a part-time job." Terri wise cracked and immediately regretted it.

****

Terri and Vanessa stood at the head of the path between Vanessa Vaughn's and Lola May's properties with Rody. Terri and Vanessa, independently of each other, assumed Rody was short for Rodent. His eyes were extremely close together, divided by a blade thin nose that was pierced. He had a tattoo possibly up from his feet to his chin. His pimples had pimples. A thoroughly repellant fellow with the body of a cartoon weight lifter, thanks to steroids, Rodent met all of Vanessa Vaughn's requirements.

Terri had only herself to blame for this. Vanessa had latched onto the idea of scaring people away from the path ever since Terri mentioned it at the detention center. Without the gate, Vanessa was convinced they were all in imminent peril. And, though plenty scary, Herman could not be persuaded to patrol the path. Over the years, the Mays and the Vaughns had both tried to convince Herman to take up security work and even succeeded once, a long time ago. Terri didn't have specifics, but it didn't end well. Herman "the Monster" became a challenge to the youths of Palm Beach instead of a deterrent. With this security void to fill, Vanessa was even more determined to take their mandatory community service to a whole new level of righteousness.

"This is the rehabilitation and detention center. We've been sent here to rehabilitate," Vanessa told Terri.

"What? No. We've been sent here to be rehabilitated," Terri argued.

"No, dear. We must do all we can to rehabilitate the less fortunate."

"I'm a less fortunate," Terri argued again.

Vanessa remained determined to rehabilitate an actual criminal. It didn't matter how many times Terri pointed out THEY were actual criminals serving MANDATORY community service sentences themselves. Vanessa was relentless. She would have her way if she had to wear Terri down to dust to get it, and she selected Rodent as their ideal "rehabilitate-ee." He was on parole and wore an ankle monitor. Vanessa had been instructing him for the past half hour.

"I gotta stand here. Look mean," Rodent clarified his duties and smiled, showing broken, yellow teeth. He couldn't believe all this easy money. Or how dumb these chicks were.

"Yes. That's all. Don't hurt anyone just look, you know, discouraging," Vanessa told him in her authoritarian clench. Terri thought the chances of this turning out like Vanessa hoped were nil. Rodent probably understood less than half the words Vanessa spoke and, for sure, he hadn't been detained at the Everglades Detention Center for nothing.

"Where's my fuckin' money?" Rodent wanted to know. "Also, where's them dumb dogs I saw earlier?"

Rodent had developed a real taste for abusing animals as a kid and never missed an opportunity to torture a defenseless creature, then watch it cower and suffer. The bigger, the better. As soon as Rodent saw Vanessa Vaughn's big, old golden retrievers, he decided he was going to douse them with gas and set them on fire. That gave him the biggest charge of anything: burning creatures alive. He used to have a friend who ran a dog fighting club, and sometimes he'd let him burn the loser. Rodent was getting excited just thinking about it.

"I told you half now and the other half tomorrow morning. And don't think you can sneak off and come back later, hmm?" Vanessa scolded Rodent in advance. "I'm paying you to guard this path the whole time."

Terri had a terrible feeling about this.

CHAPTER 18

TERRI WORE HER very best suit—her only suit. The skirt slid around sideways because it was too big. The hem hung longer on the left side than the right side, and the suit was dated. Yet, somehow, on Terri it worked. It went with her disheveled hair. Mostly Terri liked the color, a mossy green, and that gave her confidence. She had high hopes for Lola May's house, and she'd put together a killer presentation to support it. She'd already sat through two hours of other petitioners. All of their petitions had been granted with less than ten minutes of deliberations. Terri knew her petition was infinitely better than any of theirs.

When her turn came to present to the Palm Beach Historic Landmarks and Preservation Board, Terri set up her easel and her notes. She laser focused on speaking calmly and clearly. Terri had made stunning drawings of Lola May's house to illustrate her presentation, including the former terraced room.

Terri brought edifying old photographs, a survey and a plat map, and had more than a dozen precedents gathered from the internet to support Lola May's petition.

"In conclusion," Terri said, "We seek approval to restore Mrs. May's terraced room to historic accuracy under the grandfather provision."

KA-CHING Terri silently cheered. Forget about selling the columns separately from the house. That was small potatoes. Terri had made an iron-clad case for restoring the whole terraced room. The room would protect the priceless, antique columns and restore Lola May's house to its former glory. Most importantly, it would add an additional 1,800 square feet, and Lola May's would jump up from a $16 million dollar listing to a $20 million dollar listing. *KA-CHING*. Her heart sang at the prospect.

Terri gathered up her pictures and notes and her easel. She was sure they'd give her approval. There wasn't one thing they could possibly object too. It wasn't even east of the coastal construction line. The literal line in the sand, east of which the army corps of engineers would not allow construction. The coastal whatever, was the death of many an oceanfront project. Terri sat herself in the audience's front row, awaiting the board's verdict. They were in a very small auditorium inside Palm Beach's pretty town hall. The Palm Beach Historic Landmarks and Preservation Board sat in leather armchairs behind a long polished table on a shallow stage. They conferred in whispers among themselves between each petitioner before coming to their decisions. Now that Terri's pitch was behind her and she wasn't nervous as a cat, she really looked at the board members individually.

She'd recognized jowly Judge Montgomery right off. He could be a problem even though he looked right through her on the two occasions they'd met. Terri also recognized Linda Berens, the commissioner's wife, and then immediately confused her with another women board member sitting two seats away. The commissioner's smug wife was nearly indistinguishable from not one, but two, other women seated up there. They were all blonde, thin, and super-fit. They were all too tan, and they wore too-short dresses and Jack Rogers sandals. They had too-similar faces.

For a second, Terri thought she saw smarmy Brinker Deeley too: the hair-flicking pudge of a realtor who'd shown up out of nowhere with a suspiciously low offer for Lola May's house and then pretended not to know her at all at the Bath & Racquet Club. It would totally be in his best interest to deny the petition, keeping Lola's house small and less expensive. But, on closer examination, Terri realized it wasn't Brinker, and she was getting herself worked up for nothing.

Still, what was with this committee? There were like, three Lindas and five Brinker look-a-likes. Red faced, bloated, necks bulging over their pastel collars? Am I on a surprise game show? Terri thought.

"Don't I know you?" *Oh shit.* Judge Montgomery spied Terri. She liked him better in a golf beanie. "You look mighty, uh, familiar."

"I get that a lot," Terri said, trying to hide her face with her hair.

"Was there something you wanted to add, Ms. Somerville? I can't imagine there could be. You were exhaustive," Linda Berens said insultingly and with unwarranted impatience.

"No?" Terri said. "Are you granting Mrs. May's petition?"

"We'll discuss it at the next full committee meeting. We'll have to take a vote on the matter; then we will let you know," Linda Berens, the commissioner's wife, said.

"Really? Because you voted on all the other petitions I saw today, today," Terri said.

"I beg your pardon? Are you questioning this board's procedures?" Linda Berens asked, incredulously.

"Pardon me. When is the next full committee meeting?" Terri asked, wisely biting her tongue.

"The full committee meets every September," Linda said. Then she spoke to the room at large. "Thank you all very much for your efforts today. We've done some marvelous work here, and I make a motion to adjourn."

"Whoa, wait. September? Please. This is time sensitive. And, as everyone here knows, Mrs. May is not a young woman."

Linda cut Terri off, "Are you suggesting we discriminate? That is not our concern. Your petition will be addressed in due course."

"But you just granted some developer before me his petition to rip down everything but the front door of an historic library. We're only trying to put an original room back." Terri protested. "A tiny, tiny room."

"I think we've heard enough from you, miss. I second Linda's motion to adjourn," Judge Montgomery said.

There was a collective, "Here, here," from the board. They all stood up and began chatting amongst themselves and collecting their belongings.

What the hell just happened? Terri couldn't believe they just shut down her whole petition—at least until it wouldn't matter anymore to the sale price.

CHAPTER 19

LOLA MAY WAS enthroned at her dining room table, sipping gin and stirring chandelier crystals in a bowl of soapy water. She'd been humming happily to herself all morning until Joel arrived. Joel was carrying a huge cardboard box he could barely see around. At the front door he tried to brace the box on the door to knock, but it was unlatched and was pushed open. He stepped inside.

"Hello? Terri? Helloooo?" Joel called out. Lola instantly stopped humming.

"Oh, oh my, oh my, oh my." Lola said. Joel heard the breathy exclamations coming from down the hall and wandered carefully in that direction. He really couldn't see anything over the box and navigated by looking down and to the side, hoping there wasn't an obstacle in front of him. He stopped at the dining room archway and called out again.

"Hello? Excuse me. I'm Joel. These are for Terri." Joel listened but heard only silence on the other side of his box. "They're lights," Joel continued. "Christmas lights. Y'know, Santa, eggnog, those kind." Joel gave the box a little rattle.

"Oh my, oh my, oh my word." Lola breathily squeaked.

Terri came racing in from outside where she'd been staking off the former terraced room. Ever since the Palm Beach Historic Preservation and Landmarks Board had shut down her petition, Terri was determined to expand the square footage of Lola's house and the price she could get for it. *How dare those sanctimonious bureaucrats louse up Lola's sale price.* And she'd be damned if she'd let that smug tub Brinker Deeley's lowball offer win the day.

Terri had gone straight from her petitioning at Town Hall to Premium Property Partners' lawyer's offices. She'd caught one of the attorneys in the elevator on their way home for the day. She'd been PPP's lawyer for many years and was used to Terri's lack of preamble.

Without even a hello, Terri said, "I petitioned the Palm Beach Historic Preservation and Landmarks Board of Directors today for a variance on an historic landmark. They refused to decide on it until September. September. September. Here's my question—can I legally say that this variance is pending? Like you could say about a patent? Patent pending? Variance pending?" Terri asked and then exuberantly hugged the woman attorney when she told Terri, yes, she could. Now Terri had a plan and, with Joel's help, it could work. She turned back to Lola.

"Lola. I'm so sorry. This is Joel, our office manager. I didn't know he was coming by."

"I didn't know we had an office," Lola replied.

"Oh. Now you know." Terri steered Joel into the hall.

He whispered to Terri, "Damn. I'm sorry. I think I brought on some kind of fit."

"Eggnog gives you gas." Lola shouted from the dining room.

"She's fine," Terri said and looked in the giant box Joel carried. "The lights. You're brilliant. Thank you." Terri led Joel out the front door. They detoured to Joel's car so Terri could haul another box of Xmas lights. His trunk was full of them. They carried their loads around to the backyard. Terri had telescoping pipe set at intervals on the lawn designating the former, and hopefully future, terraced room. Her friend Molly ran a party rental company and loaned the pipe to her. Sometime during the night Herman would stake the pipe into the ground. He was very Hans Christian Anderson-y that way. He only came out at night.

Terri and Joel planned to string the Xmas lights from pole to pole and thread them through the petrified bougainvillea canopies Herman left jutting out four feet past the roof line at Terri's behest. She and Joel considered that it would be much brighter inside the house if they cut the vines away completely but decided to leave them. Neither Lola's ancient air conditioner nor Terri's frantic faux and touch-up painting would be improved by more heat or more light.

"I'll leave the rest of the lights by the front door for now. And I almost forgot," Joel said. He handed Terri a big, glossy magazine that had been wedged into the box he carried. "Here it is."

"Here what is?"

"Don't you check your messages?" Joel asked and flipped the magazine over. "This came out this morning."

It was *Palm Beach Society Magazine*: the big, glossy, oversized tabloid absolutely everyone in Palm Beach read cover to cover.

The whole back cover was one of Terri's sketches from her petition to the Historic Landmark Board. There was a headline. It read:

Live the Dream—First Time Ever on the Market—The May Estate: Premium Property Partners Real Estate. Contact Terri Somerville: #561-266-0778.

"Anthony and Angelo sprang for this?" Terri couldn't believe it.

"Angelo insisted on the back cover. For the next issue too. He's got visions of a sold sign splashed all over it. You're the golden girl around the office now. June Alice is out of her mind with jealousy. How's Herman?" Joel asked.

"Amazing. We have a system. I sketch out exactly what I want him to do and leave it by the pool for him to find at night. Then, the next morning, I get a surprise. Come see." Terri took Joel's hand and dragged him down one of the many tunnels Herman had carved out of the surrounding jungle. They were bent over double because the tunnel was only four feet high. A minute later, with Joel complaining of cramping up, they came to a small clearing, like they'd walked into a teepee hollowed out of a rain forest. They could even stand up in the center.

"All right—" Joel asked, looking around the small, random space.

"Not exactly what I was going for. I was trying to get him to clear a wider perimeter around the house. But he worked so hard. And was so proud of himself when he showed me I couldn't tell him that's not what I wanted. I think they're kind of neat."

"How many are there?" Joel asked.

"Five, so far. Don't worry; they're not noticeable. And who would creep through here except us? There's snakes."

"I hate you." Joel screeched and ran from the tunnel with Terri's laughter following him. She caught up with him in the driveway. He said, "You better hustle up. Angelo will have a cow if you're late to-night. I think he wants to show you off."

"What, tonight?" Terri asked.

"Palm Beach County Sherriff's Gala. The most important social networking event of the season, dearie. Where local old money and foreign new money come to play 'mines bigger than yours.' It's the Target on Crime Gala," Joel said.

"You're making that up," Terri was aghast.

"God as my witness."

"That's just wrong."

"You won't get an argument from me. Anthony and Angelo paid a fortune for a table right up front," Joel said.

"Even for Palm Beach that's awful. Might as well call it the 'Kill the Criminals Gala.'" Terri said.

"That's next year's," Joel said.

CHAPTER 20

Unbelievable. Terri thought.

IT REALLY WAS the Target on Crime Gala. There was a giant, flowered banner, like you'd see at a funeral, laid over a casket spelling out "SHERIFF'S TARGET ON CRIME GALA" in red, white, and blue carnations. The gala was being held at the Breakers Grand Resort Hotel in their most enormous ballroom. There was a full color guard representing the armed services and a Marine Corp band on parade playing Susa. Because the event was heavy on self-aggrandizement with many recognitions, awards, and speeches coming from around the room, the lights were set way up, like a Little League night game. Terri worked to keep her expression neutral throughout the sensory assault.

"Terri, stop that," Anthony or Angelo scolded her.

"Stop what?"

"Stop making that face," he said. Terri had been watching a women in a bejeweled evening gown giddily play Shoot the Prisoner. It was the classic, full-size Shoot the Duck gallery game, only the metal ducks had been replaced with black metal prisoners. A red and white bullseye had been painted on their chests. It was part of a fundraising effort and was set up on the stage. Tonight's guests were in a frenzy to pay $200 bucks a pop to have a go at it. They were lining up. Terri guessed whoever shot the most prisoners probably won something atrocious, like a game hunting safari.

"I thought I was smiling," Terri said and tried harder to not look horrified or burst out laughing. She was seated at the Premium Property Partners table. As usual, Anthony and Angelo had worn the same tuxedo and bow tie so they could not be properly identified. One of them sat next to her. Otis, a sixty-five-year-old retired golf pro who specialized in golf communities sat on Terri's other side. He was a giant teddy bear of a man who spoke much too loudly and was deaf as a post.

"Terri, did you ever get over that yeast infection thing you had?" Otis shouted beside her.

The detested June Alice was seated across the table from Terri. Her husband sat beside her. Terri was happy to see June Alice outweighed him by fifty pounds and she wore the same gown as four other women there. It had been in all the magazines adorning sixteen-year-old, six-foot-tall wraiths. It was brown and slinky and screamed "I'm-a-Gucci" with its interlocking red and green Gs all over it. It looked hilariously bad.

The table directly behind Terri was reserved for the very old and prestigious Island Title and Real Estate Company. They referred to themselves as "an old Island company." As in, call us if you'll be on the island; otherwise, don't bother. The Palm Beach was a given, and they never failed to distinguish it from West Palm Beach: literally a thirty-second drive over the bridge. The Island Title and Realty Company alone kept snobbery alive and well in Palm Beach.

They found their seats directly behind Terri, and Sally Title leaned her giant horse face nearly into Terri's soup, which looked delicious. And Terri was starving.

"Is this she?" Sally Title demanded of Anthony or Angelo. Sally was fourth generation Island Title and Realty and her sense of entitlement knew no bounds. She was a heavy, square jawed, fifty-something born into great wealth, who never for one moment thought her favor was curried for any reason beyond her own wonderfulness. She was wearing an ill-advised, strapless, red gown. She spoke like Vanessa, and she was playfully, yuck, leaning backward into Terri's soup.

"Yes, Sally. This is Terri Somerville. She's our agent of the hour," Anthony or Angelo said, then completed the introduction.

"Terri, this is Sally of Island Title and Realty. I was telling Sally what a treasure you've unearthed in the May Estate."

"Congratulations. The May House is quite a listing for someone like you," Sally said. *Someone like me?* Terri thought, but wisely said nothing. Sally continued, "I may have a buyer. But you know May House is terribly small—with its landmark and so terribly public with its path from the road to the beach—you can't expect any *real* money for it," Sally pronounced.

"But I still terribly do," Terri said. Anthony or Angelo interrupted her.

"Sally, I'll make sure you get invitations to the preview party, and if you want to bring your buyer by sooner, Terri will be happy to show it to you."

"No, I won't." Terri protested. Mrs. May's house looked amazing, particularly compared to when Terri took the listing two weeks ago, but these last days of tweaking with Joel would make all the difference. Joel was proving to be worth his weight in gold. He was the one who suggested verandaizing the overhanging shrub with tiny, soft white lights, and he was the one who had art-directed the endless decluttering of the house.

Just past Otis's shoulder, Terri saw none other than Vanessa Vaughn heading toward her. *C'mon, why? Not tonight.* Terri prayed silently and crouched down in her seat as low as she possibly could using Otis as a big, jolly shield.

"Are you alright? What is she doing?" Sally Title wanted to know.

"Terri, what are you doing?" Anthony/Angelo wanted to know. Vanessa passed by harmlessly, unaware of Terri's presence. "People are staring." Anthony/Angelo snapped.

Terri stayed low and watched Vanessa's progress through the room, lest Vanessa turn around and spot her. She saw lots of those similarly faced people in the crowd from the Historic Preservation and Landmarks Board petition. *Or maybe they were from the Preservation Society luncheon or maybe from prison?* And they were all scowling at her. At her. All pink and peevish and totally giving Terri the stink eye. *Huh?*

"Are you all right?" Sally Title asked.

"I'm—paranoid," Terri answered and shrank even further back in her chair. Suddenly Robert's face appeared beside her and Terri had to stifle a *SHRIEK*.

"Terri? It's me, Robert. Joel's stepbro? This is really a surprise running into you here. I meant to call you, tell you we got off on the wrong foot."

"I know," Terri said.

"But hey, this is really lucky. I don't fly out until noon tomorrow."

"Really?" Terri said. Robert checked his watch.

"Yes. Damn. I can't ditch these people I came with yet. But I can meet later."

"You can?" *Is he this dumb?* Terri thought.

"You bet," Robert said.

Guess so. "Okay." Terri said, "You can meet—Otis. But why wait? Otis, this is Robert."

"How ya doing?" Otis boomed and crushed Robert's hand in his giant paw.

"You'll *love* him," Terri assured Robert as she stood up. "You can hear him from really far away."

And Terri left Robert with his hand safely trapped in Otis's beefy paw and wandered out of the main ballroom into the reception area. It was crowded with guests tricked out in designer clothing. Everyone was struggling to be seen. To be heard. To get a drink at the bar Terri was aiming toward. She moved slowly with the current until she joined the cue at the bar and became engulfed in a cloud of too much conflicting perfume. Terri wasn't alone coughing her way to the head of the line.

"What'll it be?" the bartender asked. *Oh shit*, Terri thought, *what are the odds?* Tending bar was the charred home inspector, Darryl. Guess he moonlighted as a bartender. He had apparently shaved the other side of his face and head to match what was singed off because he was uniformly furry again, except for his hands. One looked waxed and the other like a mouse was sitting on it. Maybe Terri wasn't getting that drink after all. She kept her head down and tried to disguise her voice.

"A glass of vodka over ice, please?"

"Hey, it's you. The lunatic. You clean up nice," Darryl said.

"Thanks—how's your weasel?" Terri asked.

"You mean my ferret? Great. I think you really captured him. No pun intended. Huh, huh. Anyways, I hung his portrait up over his cage. Looks great. Here you go. It's on me." Terri took the drink from him and knocked it back where she stood.

"Another?" Terri squeaked as the drink burned its way down.

"Sure," Darryl said and fixed her another. Terri took the drink and wandered over to the silent auction area where all the auction items and prizes were displayed. Gala guests bid for art and jewels and cars and trips and holiday homes. Terri idly picked up a fancy, glossy brochure from a stack on the display table. And, dear God, the guest who shot the most prisoners really did win an African big-game hunting safari. It was enough to make Terri cue up in the noxious bar line for another vodka.

CHAPTER 21

TERRI DROPPED HER keys on a growing pile of bills and magazines. She pushed play on her answering machine while she changed into running clothes and hunted for her sneakers.

BEEP. Terri was greeted with a strong New York accented smoker's voice.

"This is Harriet Nussbaum with Waterfront Properties Realty. What is this May Estate? Whaaat? The price is too high I can tell you that right now. I'm calling because I'll be at the preview party." *CLICK.*

Can't wait to meet her, Terri thought.

BEEP. The next message was from Joel. "It's me. More good news. Your bible people dropped a contract by the office. Congratulations and God bless."

Terri could hear Joel giggling before he hung up.

BEEP. "Terri, this is June Alice. I've been taking messages for you all day long. They're all waiting on your desk, so you better go to the office. I finally had to give out your home phone to whomever called because your cell is no longer accepting messages. That's so unprofessional. It's not my fault you're not prepared for your open house, and it's not my job to screen your calls."

June Alice, you're such an ass.

BEEP. "Hello, Terri? Weldon Blakely here. I'm RSVPing for the Island Southeby's Affiliates. There'll be seventeen of us attending."

Of course there'll be seventeen of you, you entitled twits, Terri snorted to herself.

BEEP. "Dis is Joey Maccetti. Prudential. I gotta buyer comin' wit me to your open house in Palm Beach. You're servin' drinks and shit, right? Any food? 238-6363. 954 area code."

There was a fifty-fifty chance Joey turned up with a legit buyer and a fifty-fifty chance he brought a hooker.

BEEP. "Alert. Are you paying too much for life insurance? Go on line to www—dot benefit forever—dot com for savings you can't live without." said a canned voice.

BEEP. "You have no more messages," said the machine.

"No more messages," Terri mimicked. The cute detective, E. Shay, had not called. *Jerk.* Terri glared at the answering machine then stabbed erase so hard she knocked it into the growing pile she'd tossed her keys on and the whole heap slid to the floor.

There, on top, was the brochure for the African hunting safari prize. So revolting. It offered a wonderful world of slaughtering magnificent animals in the wild while the natives waited on you hand and foot and stood sentry with rifles. Guests slept in luxurious tents with air conditioning, flat screen TVs, and marble baths.

Wait, what?

Terri grabbed up the brochure. Her heart started to pound. How could she not have realized this sooner? She started to call Joel and hung up. She should call Molly, her party rental pal, first. Her mind was flying in a million directions. Could it be done? Was there even enough time? Terri grabbed her keys and raced for the door, then dashed back to grab a red pencil. On her way out, she added a pimple to the portrait she'd done of Detective E. Shay. It was standing on an easel beside her front door. Terri gave him a new zit each day he hadn't called. She had no real expectation that he would. Still, it was extremely satisfying to make him become less attractive as time went on.

CHAPTER 22

MONDAY AFTERNOON WAS Vanessa and Terri's second community service session, and it seemed like their hundredth to Terri. She was dead on her feet. Terri and Joel had been working on Lola May's house round the clock. Ever since, she'd really looked at that safari brochure. On top of that, Joel insisted Terri do an additional series of watercolors of the May Estate, only depicted moving forward in time instead of backward like the sketches she'd already done for the Historic Preservation and Landmarks Board petition. Those turned out to be much more difficult to paint because she wasn't mindlessly copying anything. But the intense effort was definitely worth it because of how much was at stake.

Now Terri was physically and creatively spent. She'd just finished the series of six watercolors right before she'd driven out to the Rehabilitation and Detention Center. A mind-numbing drive in and of itself but particularly this afternoon with two tractor trailer accidents on I-95 causing bumper-to-bumper traffic, adding an extra forty minutes to Terri's commute.

Take that, Timmy the Turd. Terri thought vindictively about her ex-husband. *I may be a crappy artist, but these six watercolors are going to make me more money than everything you ever stole from me combined.* Terri envisioned him shabby and hunched, boarding a Greyhound bus with nothing but a paper bag holding all his worldly belongings.

And then I would ride by Tim, mounted on a white horse. No—in a shiny, new convertible. No—she'd be carried on a throne like Cleopatra. Wait-no. Cleopatra had that snake hat on her head. And she died of an asp bite, right? What the hell am I even thinking about? C'mon Terri, get a grip. she scolded herself. *Snap out of it, girlie, and pay attention to the here and now. Think of where you are. Get alert.*

She and Vanessa were back in their same rehab classroom. Vanessa, again with the pearls and behatted. Terri came prepared. On the way there she told Vanessa, in a pathetic, rasping whisper, that she'd lost her voice and Vanessa would have to read the pamphlets aloud this time. Fortunately, Vanessa agreed and took charge. It was mostly the same detainees as before, with a few exceptions.

Vanessa was at her most unbearably patronizing, and not for the first time Terri channeled Lola's invisible trick for all she was worth. But that much delusion was unachievable, at least without alcohol and meds. Terri tuned Vanessa out and surveyed the prisoners in their class, then immediately wished she hadn't. They were a sorry group. They scratched their balls and picked their noses. They coughed up globs of phlegm and spat them on the floor. A couple had frightening, nervous tics. One poor soul had a convulsion and the guards had to come in and haul him off. They all smelled like they'd been rolling in sewage, and Terri breathed through her mouth to keep from gagging. *When would this end?* she thought and then tuned into what Vanessa was saying again.

"I've taken it upon myself to bring in my own copy of Emily Post's *Book of Etiquette*. It's a second edition, and I'll expect you to handle it with the care it's due, hmm?"

Oh my God. Really, Vanessa? Are you serious? "They will throw it at us—" Terri hissed at Vanessa. "Please Mrs. Vaughn, I think we should just read the pamphlets."

"Shut up, ya old bag." one shouted.

"Shut up. Hmm." shouted his homeless, drug-addicted friend. God help Terri, he had mimicked Vanessa perfectly.

Shit, shit. Terri burst into laughter. She couldn't stop it. She gasped and shook and laughed so hard she couldn't catch her breath. She thought she might actually die laughing. The guards outside became alarmed enough to burst in again. One of them patted Terri soothingly on the back, thinking she was crying, which made her laugh harder. That and everyone's expressions. And that Vanessa had continued talking, oblivious.

"I will have you know that this Emily Post *Book of Etiquette* has just as much relevance today as it did when I was a young woman."

A person Terri assumed to be a prostitute in a leopard spandex cat suit and Lady Godiva wig lurched to her feet, objecting. "You weren't never young. Talkin' that revelance shit. Revelance. Speak English, you dumb bitch."

"Excuse me, my English?" Vanessa looked like her head would explode. "You dare to question my command of the English language? Your speech is incomprehensible. Your manners are despicable, and you have only the most rudimentary vocabulary." Vanessa's teeth must be ground to nubs by now. She continued, red-faced. "Where do you people live? In a barn?"

This sent everyone into peals of laughter. Somehow the "homelessness" part of the homeless hadn't registered with Vanessa.

Then they started answering back.

"Where I live?" the drunk prostitute sang out. "I'm a-livin' in the past. We all live in the past." For some reason, this was hilarious.

"Shit, bitch, past is free," shouted an apparent flasher in a trench coat. "Dumb bitch don't know shit." They were all shouting by then. Except the gangs, who were strangely caucusing among themselves.

Not good, Terri thought.

"Oh please. There's no reason why any of you can't become functioning members of society." Vanessa was yelling over them. *How does she get that much volume with her teeth clenched that way?* Terri thought. And crossed her arms on the table and laid her head down. Terri immediately nodded off because the next thing she knew, Vanessa was poking her awake and the last of the class was shuffling out the door.

"I thought that went rather well, don't you, hmm?"

CHAPTER 23

IT WAS 4:00 P.M. and seventeen days since Terri was first summoned to the May Estate for what she thought was a restoration job. It had kind of turned into one too. Usually, when Terri took a new real estate listing (especially one for so short a time), she had it listed in the multiple listing service that day with the photographs and virtual tour executed and posted online the next. Unless there was a weather delay, which was always annoying.

But Lola May's was an oceanfront, historic landmark. There was a formula for what this size oceanfront parcel of land would be worth, minus a trifecta of drawbacks. One: a government easement along one boundary. Two: a commercial country club along the other. Three: Lola May's historic landmarked house. The latter was the only drawback Terri could do something about. Seventeen days ago, Terri arrived at an overgrown, neglected ruin that could not be torn down, altered, or expanded. Her task had been to make Lola May's house appear as appealing, spacious, and valuable as possible to the widest pool of buyers. Right now, even she was amazed at what they'd accomplished in so short a time.

Oh my God, Terri thought, suddenly nervous and a bit overwhelmed with everything that was happening. *I have a terrified, agoraphobic seller. And a monster on the premises. Two, if you count Vanessa. And two identical bosses, loaded with expectations. And as long as I'm counting, I've got a huge crush on a guy I'll probably never see again. But I'm not giving a shit about that because, holy shit, if everything goes perfectly right tonight I'll have a twenty million dollar listing. Hee hee, ha ha. And a two hundred and forty thousand dollar commission. Not all mine, but still. Too bad the sixteen million dollar mortgage owed Whitney Bank is exempt. The bastards.*

At Joel's insistence, Terri wore an extremely uncomfortable dress he bought for her at a consignment shop. It was a fancy designer frock and there was a label digging into her back. The whole form-fitting contraption strangled her from neck to knees. But Joel assured her she looked good: like she sold $20 million dollar properties every day of the week.

I could pay off my credit cards, get a new car, reduce my mortgage. She paused, then thought, *Wait, what if I turn into a Republican?*

"Quit tugging on that. You're stretching it out of shape," Joel scolded, snapping Terri out of her musings. They were standing in Lola May's front courtyard. It was all cleared and freshly laid with bright white pebbles. Terri was briefing Angelo/Anthony and the rest of the Pee Pee Pee-ers before the guests arrived for the grand preview reception.

Terri was dragging her presentation out because she and Joel were ahead of schedule.

"It's supposed to be clingy. Leave it alone," Joel told her.

"No one's looking at you, Terri. They're coming to view Mrs. May's house. Stop trying to make yourself the center of attention and get on with it," June Alice spat.

Terri ignored her and continued. "Everyone please do not, do NOT, try to turn anything on. Nothing is connected. We have the house and grounds pre-lit to their best advantage already. And please don't charge your phones. There's barely electricity," Terri said. She turned to Joel. "What else?"

Joel glanced over his shoulder. "Herman."

"Right. Over there?" Terri pointed at the dense jungle looming close to the house on the north side of the property. "Deep in there stands a utility shed you can't see. It's Herman's shed. Do not go near there. Stay away from that." *Because Herman will scare you to death. And his shed is so stuffed with Lola's furniture it could burst tester bed shrapnel far and wide at the smallest provocation.*

As soon as the Safari Company agreed to do it, Terri, Joel, Mrs. Irish, and Herman hauled all of the bedroom furniture out of the house and crammed it into Herman's shed. Overnight, Lola May's had gone from a small, decrepit landmark to a huge six bedroom estate. One master bedroom and five individual, ultra-luxury tent bedrooms with teak floors, king sized beds, air conditioning, flat screen TVs, marble baths, and bars. Each had teak verandas and five-star hotel furnishings.

"The beauty of the tents," Terri couldn't help but boast, "is they can be taken down and stored for hurricane season, so they are never part of the property tax base. All the new owner needs is a permit. Each year they can erect as many or as few tents as they want. The tents can be easily reconfigured, upgraded, and modernized too. There's a series of watercolors depicting this in the upstairs gallery."

"Is this a joke?" June Alice asked. "Who would sleep in a tent? What are we, Boy Scouts? This is ridiculous."

"June Alice, please. Let's give Terri the benefit of the doubt. Terri, where are these five supposed wonder tents? I have to say, standing here, I expected to be more impressed," Angelo said.

"Follow me," Terri said. "There's one example tent set up for now." She led Angelo, June Alice, and the realtors down one of Herman's tunnels. He had cleared it to six-feet, two-inches high, so they could all walk up right to reach the teepee-shaped clearing that now held an elegant canvas tent. It was elevated two feet off the ground and had polished teak wood floors. The interior was more luxurious than any bedroom any of them had ever seen.

That's saying something for a group of realtors.

It had a built-in walnut and crystal wet bar with a fridge and an icemaker. The bathroom was all marble and included a deep, claw-footed tub and glass-enclosed shower. The tent was furnished for royalty, with priceless antiques scattered throughout. The bedding was exquisite and Italian. A large flat screen TV hung on one canvas wall, and another TV was embedded in the bathroom mirror. Terri needed to remember to turn it on before the other realtors arrived.

The Safari Company had been delighted to set up one of their luxury tents on Terri's prestigious Palm Beach oceanfront listing. It would be great publicity for them. A stack of their brochures, for their photo safaris only, lay on a beautiful glass and bamboo secretary by the tent's front door. They had stocked the bar with Ruinart champagne and the silver ice bucket with ice. An eighty-dollar scented candle had the tent smelling sublime. All the Pee Pee Pee-ers gasped in delight as they entered the tent, except for June Alice, of course, who was searching for something negative to say.

Terri preempted her, "Before we head back to see the house, remember the kitchen is off limits tonight. Do not go in there. Remember Mrs. May's in there, and we don't want to freak her out. Mrs. Irish will be guarding the door. I—I wouldn't mess with her either. Just saying." Terri looked at Joel, who consulted his watch and nodded. It was time.

Terri led her coworkers back through Herman's tunnel to the house. Again, she stopped them on the newly pebbled driveway. It was nothing less than astonishing, what they had accomplished. Herman's misunderstanding of most of Terri's directions had resulted in a truly magical transformation. The setting sun was on the verge of bathing Lola May's house in a rose gold haze.

Terri remembered the afternoon she'd spent coaxing Herman out of his shed so she could direct his pruning to let the sun shine in just this way. Terri pointed. Herman chain sawed. All went well until Herman unearthed a nest that sent him fleeing back to his shed for two days and gave Terri nightmares. The May Estate had been neglected so long it had established its own ecosystem, complete with its own evolving, feral creatures.

"This is amazing. An albino Cuban knight anole, mutated to seventy-times its usual size." exclaimed the junior Palm Beach County Animal Control technician Terri had called to exterminate the horrible creature. The technician didn't look old enough to shave. And he was beyond delirious with joy at the horror Terri was showing him. "And a nest with eggs." he cried. "This is astounding. We have to bring in someone from University of Miami's eco-research department. And the Fish and Wildlife's Protected Species Division too." Terri went a little berserk.

"We need to kill these fuckers right now." she screamed at this bewildered man/child in an animal control jumpsuit who carried a looped stick and a cage. "They're translucent snake lizards the size of Pomeranians." Terri shrieked. "And you have to kill them. Vaporize them. Yesterday. Before they spread."

"This could be the scientific discovery of a lifetime," Junior Wildlife whined.

"No, it couldn't. Because I can't get out of my car until they're gone. Do you swear on your mother's life there are no more nests or anoles like these anywhere else on Mrs. May's property?"

"Yes. I told you these are unprecedented," Junior Wildlife said.

"Swear it."

"Um, uh, Miss Terri, can you roll down your window a little? I can hardly hear you," he said.

That seemed like a lifetime ago. Terri glanced at her fellow agents gathered together and standing on the edges of the cleared perimeter, except for June Alice, who stood next to the house under the four feet of overhanging trellis.

"June Alice is standing on the West Veranda. It's nice space. Wide and naturally covered," Terri said.

"Making up fancy names isn't going to get this house sold," June Alice said.

"Terri, there has to be a better place to greet these brokers than out here in the shadows," Angelo chimed in. "Let's go inside."

"Okay," Terri said. "But all you Premium Property agents should know Joel staged this property for me. He's a design genius, and we're idiots to not use him on all of our listings," Terri endorsed her pal, hoping to get him more business.

In the next moment, the sun blazed golden across Lola's house. Every pane of glass sparkled like crystal. Terri plugged in a hidden extension cord and miles of tiny lights twinkled in the bougainvillea canopies. Joel unshrouded the defunct fountain in the center of the pebbled circular drive to reveal a riot of cascading scarlet and fuchsia flowers tumbling down its sides. Because Herman had carved each tunnel at a different height, like lollipops on varied length sticks, this magic hour lighting would continue for the next seventy minutes, until the sun set.

Everybody better damn well be prompt. Terri thought.

After dark, artfully placed torches, candles, and more twinkly lights would flatter the place as much as could be hoped for—and way more than in daylight. Terri and Joel did a little victory dance while everyone gasped in awe.

Everyone, except June Alice. She was still standing against the house under a broad canopy of petrified bougainvillea intertwined with teeny white lights.

"June Alice, that's a really bad place to stand." *There,* Terri thought. *I told her.* June Alice looked around.

"You're telling me where to stand? I'm a professional. I know how to show a house. And I don't have to resort to cheap theatrics to do it."

"Okay," Terri said and shook her head. *Bad Terri.* Terri looked up at the canopy above June Alice's head. "The lizards don't like these lights."

"So, why should I care? The lizards aren't my clients."

"No. They're lizards."

Right then, in ones, then twos, then tens, sticky, brown lizards the size of cigarettes leapt from the canopy above June Alice and rained down on her head. They made sharp, squeaky croaks and tangled in June Alice's hair.

Shit. Terri thought, *I'm laughing too hard to film this for YouTube.* June Alice screamed like she was on fire and swatted spastically at her own face and head, like some kind of demented end-zone dance. Terri almost pissed herself.

"June Alice. Get a hold of yourself." Anthony ordered. "People are arriving."

And they were. All at once. Leave it to realtors to take full advantage of any offered free food and drinks. It was turning into an early crush, and Joel and Terri still had torches and candles to fire up and flowers to place out back and on the bar. There was white wine, vodka, or water only and snack tables; mayonnaise & watercress tea sandwiches; celery and carrots with cucumber dip served in a hollowed-out cabbage; and the best teeny-weenie, Palm Beach cheese puffs. Caterers would pass those and other tiny morsels around on sticks.

June Alice kept dancing around in Terri's head, and Terri kept snorting back bursts of laughter. She hoped everyone just thought she was crying. Sally Title shoved her horse face right in front of Terri.

"Sally Title, Island Title and Realty. You remember me. This really is a hidden jewel. When we spoke at the Sheriff's Gala I was sure your asking price was pie in the sky."

Terri squeaked out a dry, "Nope."

"Yes, so I see. There's still that public path running along the northern boundary. I saw it wasn't gated. But the house is grand. I love the spa and salon upstairs."

Joel had ingeniously hauled a shampoo sink into one of the empty bedrooms upstairs and styled it with another empty bedroom and connecting bath as a chic salon-spa suite. Two more emptied upstairs bedrooms had adjoining French doors between them. Joel removed the doors, creating one bright, grand spacious room. He called it the Cyber Library. It had black walnut floors that were freshly waxed and gleaming and had white Venetian plastered walls that glowed. A lone Lucite table stood in the center of the room, holding a kindle and a slender vase of leaves.

"Excuse me," was the best response Terri could choke out. Not even eager realtors swarming Lola May's house, talking about potential buyers and how it was unexpectedly spacious, could squash this fit of hilarity. Even remarks like, "It was stunning and immediately livable." *Immediately livable? Until you tried to turn anything on.* Neither the flat TVs nor any of the other electronics staged throughout the house were connected. And Joel had stripped the house almost bare, leaving just the most minimal and exquisite furnishings. It was livable if you didn't mind standing. *Ah oh*, Terri thought. *Please don't do that.*

The crush of realtors kept brushing against the edge of the stairs as they passed each other in the hall, near the still wet edge of the stairs Terri painted yesterday. With car enamel. At ass height. Speaking of ass, there was the fat hair-flicker himself, realtor Brinker Deeley. Terri saw he had a paint smear across his seersucker-encased arse.

****

Brinker shoved his way through the throng of realtors down the hall, past the dining room to the back staircase where no one else was. He ducked behind the stairs and crouched, trying to keep his bulk from view. Brinker mopped his sweaty brow. His hank of flicking hair was stuck to it, even though it wasn't that hot outside. He furtively pulled his cellphone from his pocket. He dialed a number then, unable to flick, bit his cuticles while he waited for his call to be answered. Brinker had been feeling extremely put-upon lately. He was sick of living in West Palm Beach. It was supposed to be for a year. Tops. And already, he knew it would be more than that. Brinker found it increasingly humiliating. He should have just rented a dump on the island, like his daughter Muffy had wanted him to. Whoever Brinker was calling picked up on the twentieth ring.

"You said it was unsalvageable. You said $2 million tops. This bitch will get ten," Brinker hissed into his phone. "This one was supposed to be mine," he continued. Brinker listened for a minute. "But everything's changed. No one cares about the easement. Or the club."

Brinker listened some more, gnawing on a hangnail. "Then meet me there right now. Both of you. You can see for yourself what she did."

Brinker hung up. He forged his way back through the crush of realtors, out the dining room doors, through the enormous, terraced room, delineated by twinkle lights where Terri had set up the bar, and continued down toward the beach. He jostled a woman he passed, splashing her drink across her chest. She was wearing an elaborately veiled hat.

"Watch out," Brinker mumbled rudely and kept going.

****

The woman wiped her blouse with a crumpled cocktail napkin that wasn't up to the task, and her soaked silk blouse clung to her huge fake boobs. She saw Terri walk by with a tray of sandwiches and followed her to the foyer. She gripped Terri's arm and whispered urgently in her ear.

"This is difficult place to speak, but I zee now in zee papers, you are an important real estate person."

Terri looked around. "Me? Are you talking to me?"

"And you are from zee West Palm Beach. That is why we saw you for the looking of apartments. This is zee most important thing because nobody must know." Terri flicked up the woman's veil for a peek, and the woman quickly pulled it back down.

"Ursula? I mean, Mrs. Lurie?" *What the heck was Mrs. Lurie doing in the middle of Terri's realtor's preview party?*

"Shhhhh. Please. You vill come to my house in zee next Tuesday, at 2:45. That is the afternoon, yes? I vill explain then all your questions." Ursula pressed an envelope into Terri's hand and hurried away.

What the hell?

CHAPTER 24

BRINKER DEELEY ALTERNATELY smeared his hank of flicking hair off his forehead and chewed his nails. He stood in the shadows where the path between Lola May's and Vanessa Vaughn's properties met the beach. He was waiting for his uncle, Judge Montgomery, and his cousin, Commissioner Scotty Berens, to show up. Brinker smelled their expensive Cuban cigars before he saw them: the really expensive cigars the judge always had on hand to share with Scotty but never with him. They walked across Lola's beach from the Bath & Racquet Club to meet Brinker.

The familial resemblance was strong. Judge Montgomery was an older, fatter version of Brinker, only without the hair-flicking and petulance. He and the comparatively gorgeous Commissioner Berens shared only a weak chin. Tonight, the judge wore a madras jacket and lime green pants with a necktie sporting little embroidered gavels. Next to him, Commissioner Scotty Berens looked especially tall and trim. He wore the blue blazer and khaki pant uniform of the entitled and a bowtie with a club insignia. The tie performed double duty, announcing Berens belonged to clubs you did not and camouflaging his weak family chin.

"Pssst, psst. Over here." Brinker whisper-shouted to them. Montgomery and Berens joined Brinker in the shadows. It was all Brinker could do to keep his tone of voice under control.

"You don't know what she did in there. There could be a bidding war. A bidding war for millions. You should have let me handle it," Brinker said.

"And brokered it to yourself? Don't be a fool," Judge Montgomery dismissed Brinker's concerns out of hand. "Before title can be transferred both the landmark status and the easement have serious legal problems to overcome. If you give me a minute here, son, I'll think of them." Judge Montgomery barked out a laugh at his own joke, har-har.

Scotty and Brinker dutifully har-harred along with him.

When? Brinker wanted to know, silently fuming. The judge and Scotty had been living in proper Palm Beach estates for years. What did they care if his deal was falling apart? They weren't stuck in West Palm Beach.

"The landmark status and easement won't matter by then. This little bitch is ruining the whole operation. We have to do something now. We can't wait." Brinker insisted. Brinker knew he was pissing his uncle off, but he was past caring.

Rodent, on path-guarding duty, stupidly chose that moment to reveal himself.

"Hey, Judge. Remember me?" Rodent announced.

"What? No. What are you doing here?" the judge demanded. Montgomery was alarmed enough to step back and behind Brinker's bulk.

"I'm working," said Rodent, swaggering forward. It would have been a more effective swagger were he not picking his nose.

"Who for?" Judge Montgomery wanted to know.

"Old lady what lives there," Rodent said, gesturing with his chin toward Vanessa Vaughn's property. "I'm guarding this here path. But I git it now. Yew-hee, Judge, I gets it. I surely do." Rodent was delighted with his own thinking and thought he was winking at the judge, but Rodent hadn't mastered winking yet. He looked like someone just threw a handful of sand in his face. "Whooo, it's just like home, ain't it, your honor?" Rodent continued with obvious glee.

Montgomery stepped forward. His good-ol'-boy drawl turned on high. He said, "Son, what's your name?"

"Rody."

"Rody, this is some fine initiative you're showing. Working all the way over here. I'm proud of you, son. Aren't you proud of him, Commissioner?"

"Indeed," Commissioner Chinless agreed.

"I bet you could use someone like Rody here on your staff. Isn't that right, Commissioner?" Judge Montgomery drawled.

"Dead right," Commissioner Scotty Berens dutifully agreed and launched into a speech about quality, available job openings, like he was an employment agency. According to the commissioner, there were all kinds of suitable positions for someone with Rody's unique qualifications that paid excellent salaries with bonuses and benefits.

"I could see you staying in security work, but what do you think about taking a job in promotions? Promotions are like the guys who drive around in the Budweiser party truck. Would you like to do that, Rody?"

Now this guy was talking Rody's language. Rody kept up with him as he ambled further up the path.

"Shit, yeah. Gots me experience too. Yeah, I'll do that," Rody told him.

Judge Montgomery shooed Brinker to follow behind and help figure out Rody's future career. The judge was going to investigate what Brinker's panic was all about back up at old Lola May's.

****

Judge Montgomery walked diagonally up from the beach across Lola's freshly mown lawn and past her magnificently tiled and sparkling pool. He walked through the twinkling illusion of the terraced room, where most of the realtors were clustered by the bar. He heard their chatter about how stunning the house was and the sheer genius of the tents. Montgomery went inside and strolled down a deceptively modest hallway that looked vast with a wall of beveled mirrors facing a wall of arched entryways. Upstairs, he saw the beautiful spa Joel invented and the even more dramatic Cyber Library. He saw Terri's water-colored series of May Estate.

The first depicted present day, with flower strewn paths leading to five private and elegant tents. The next showed Lola May's cleared and severely manicured lawn, with tents lined up facing each other like sentries on either side of a straight-center driveway, a topiary tree between each tent. The last painting in the series depicted a very sci-fi May Estate. Spaceship-like tents hovered at staggered altitudes around the property, with May House in the center like the sun. The judge had seen more than enough.

CHAPTER 25

"I COULD GET $25 MILLION DOLLARS for Lola May's. No, that's too crazy—but twenty-two? What if a buyer calls me directly? From Angelo and Anthony's ads? And I get the whole 6 percent?" Just the thought sent a tingle through Terri's whole body. In Palm Beach County real estate, the listing agent represents the seller. In an effort to sell their client's homes, listing agents typically offer 3 percent, or one-half of their own commission to the buyer's agent for delivering the buyer. If the buyer has no agent then the selling agent receives and keeps the whole 6 percent commission. "I can't believe how well everything went. Did you hear them? And the tent. It could change real estate forever. Pack-and-go luxury housing. Why didn't some-one think of this before? Joel, you totally dazzled them. Between the lights and stripping the house down. Wow. Five different agents told me they have buyers they're bringing by in the next two weeks." Terri hadn't stopped for breath. Joel was on the other end of the phone and only interrupted Terri so she wouldn't hyperventilate.

"You're babbling. I love you, but I'm exhausted," Joel said on the other end of the line.

"I know, but I'm so keyed up. Admit it. You did not expect this level of success," Terri said, triumphantly.

"Don't count your chickens, dearie. You haven't had an offer yet," Joel warned.

"Technically, that's not true. I had one really lame offer right off."

"A very lame offer, which you've already acknowledged you may have to reconsider," Joel reminded her.

"Not anymore. Not with the terraced room and the tents," Terri defended herself.

"I'm hanging up now. Kissie, kissie," said Joel.

"Wait. Joel. Did you hear that? Someone's calling me on the other line. Who would call me at this hour besides you? Maybe more congratulations from Pee Pee Pee-ers?"

****

Terri pulled into Lola May's driveway and parked behind a line of police and emergency vehicles. She walked in dread toward Lola May's house, trying hard not to speculate and give herself an anxiety attack. Terri ignored the sirens, police radio chatter, and other "crime-sceney" sounds and forced herself to put one foot in front of the other. Instead of Mrs. Irish, a female police officer met Terri at Lola's front door: Lola's paint-splattered front door.

"Are you Terri Somerville?"

"Yes?"

"Come with me, please." Instead of inviting Terri in, the officer led Terri around the outside of the house.

Why? A million questions raced through Terri's head. She hardly registered what she saw. The policewoman quickly led Terri around to the back of Lola's house toward the beach. Halfway there, Terri stopped short.

"Wait." she told the officer.

Terri took a breath and a slow survey of the house. Several of Lola's windows were smashed. All the torches and twinkle lights she could see had been ripped down or cut up. The repurposed flower fountain was destroyed. The hedges surrounding the house looked like they'd been burned.

Terri stood in stunned disbelief for endless moments, then took off at a run towards Herman's shed.

"Hey," the policewoman shouted after her. "Hey."

She shouted again and caught up with Terri outside of Herman's shed. Two firemen were prying boards off its only door. The door had been boarded and nailed shut from the outside.

"Herman." Terri shouted. "Herman."

"I don't think there's anyone in here, lady," the fireman said.

"No, he's in there. He has to be. He's just very still."

"Come on. Detective E. Shay is waiting for you at the beach," the officer said. She'd been there for hours and was getting cranky, hustling Terri along. There was a cluster of officials gathered at the water's edge, including Detective E. Shay. Terri took super slow baby steps to reach his side.

"I think we can rule out natural causes, don't you?" Shay asked Terri, almost conversationally. But she could sense he was furious. Laying, stabbed to death, in the sand at their feet was Rodent: Vanessa Vaughn's rehabilitation project. And their night watchman. Rodent. He was on his back at the water's edge. The surf floated his legs with every wave. His eyes were shut, but his mouth was open, showing those rotted, pointy, yellow teeth. There was a gaping black gash at his neck.

Terri almost burst into song she was so relieved. *Not Lola or Herman or Mrs. Irish or even Vanessa.*

Speak of the devil. Vanessa arrived just then, her golden retrievers trailing behind her. She wore a matching bathrobe ensemble, circa 1962, peered over Terri's shoulder, and said, "My dear, we shall have to find a replacement before the end of the day. Hmm?"

CHAPTER 26

VANESSA AND TERRI HAD been driven to the police station in different squad cars and placed in separate cell-like interrogation rooms. They were each seated at a table facing their own reflections in one-way mirrors. E. Shay and two other detectives were in an adjacent, viewing office between them. It was decided the interviews would be conducted via intercom, and Terri and Vanessa would be left alone for an hour of observation beforehand. As of now, they were the only connection to the deceased the police had and the reason Rody was on the premises in the first place. Taken alone, Terri and Vanessa's involvement wouldn't count for much, but there had been a fatal crash, an assault, and an electrocution at the exact same site within the past three weeks.

"You first met the victim, Rody Gouse, while performing mandatory community service at the Everglades Rehabilitation and Detention Center, after which you brought him to your home and employed him? Is that correct?" E. Shay's disembodied voice asked Vanessa Vaughn over the intercom.

"That is correct. And I must say, he was particularly repellent at the time. Ideally suited for the job. An inspired choice really," Vanessa said through clenched teeth, while sitting straight backed. Her hands were demurely folded on the table.

Terri, alone in her own tiny room, without even a pencil to doodle with, was leaping out of her skin with boredom, staring at her own reflection. *Is that something stuck between my teeth?* Terri got up, walked close to the mirror, and gave herself a full dental examination. *Look at that*, she thought, *I have a silver filling. Good to know.* Terri tore out several long strands of hair, twisted them together, and— flossed. Unbeknownst to her, there was a collective *Ewww* from the detectives on the other side of the mirror. After everyone stopped laughing, E. Shay began Terri's interview.

"Wait? What?" Terri said. E. Shay had asked Terri the same question he'd asked Vanessa about her first meeting and subsequent hiring of Rodent over the intercom. Terri instantly stopped flossing and backed away from the mirror.

"That was a bad idea. One of my worst." Terri said.

E. Shay asked, "And the last time you saw Rody?"

"He was dead," Terri said.

"Before that," E. Shay clarified

"The first night he worked for us. Vanessa spent an hour explaining to him what he was supposed to do."

"What day?" E. Shay insisted.

"I don't know. Please. I've been working round the clock, and it's all blurred together. Maybe Wednesday? One of the middle days. Thursday? Mrs. Vaughn will know," Terri said.

"Does Mrs. May have enemies?" E. Shay asked.

"Are you making a joke?"

"No."

"Okay. I can't think of anyone who'd be Lola's enemy. What about Rody? He's already a criminal," Terri suggested, helpfully.

"You and Mrs. Vaughn were at the detention center working off your own criminal charges, Terri. There have been two deaths and an assault on this property in as many weeks. How long have you been Mrs. May's realtor?" Shay asked.

"A little over two weeks? Oh shit." Terri said, than clapped her hand over her own mouth like a cartoon character.

Shit is right, E. Shay thought. Terri was probably in this up to her neck.

"Standby," E. Shay said and switched to interviewing Vanessa. He could barely get his questions out. Vanessa talked right over him.

"Of course, I didn't press charges," Vanessa said. "Herman was attacked by those spawn of the Bath & Racquet Club next door. What good would it have done? They're all some senator's nephew or the daughter of old Palm Beach money to whom everyone owes a favor. As it happens, I didn't actually see them attack Herman. I arrived afterword."

"To your knowledge, has Herman ever destroyed or vandalized May property or your own property before?" Shay asked.

"Next you'll ask me if he nailed himself shut in his own shed. Hmm? Absolutely not." Vanessa replied.

"Did he exhibit any signs of anger when he learned May House was to be sold? That he will become, in fact, homeless?" Shay asked.

"Dear," Vanessa said, indulgent. "The man barely comprehends that he is, let alone where. Leave him be."

E. Shay turned off the intercom and conferred with his fellow detectives, who were barely containing their hilarity. But they were professionals, got a grip on themselves, and concluded everyone involved bore further investigation. A fatal car crash, an electrocution, an assault, and then a murder and vandalization all on the same innocuous path was too many unfortunate incidents.

They looked at the facts:

1. Terri, Mrs. Vaughn, Rody, and the van driver had all done time at the Detention Center.

2. The site itself lead to the wide open Atlantic Ocean. A nefarious sea operation was not to be discounted. The Coast Guard would be advised.

3. The DEA would be called. E. Shay thought this was likely a drug drop gone bad. At least he hoped so. A drug drop that didn't involve Terri, even remotely.

Terri had nodded off in her small interview room. E. Shay's intercom voice woke her up. Shay asked, "Suppose you can't find a buyer for Lola May's house. What happens then?" Terri woke up slowly.

"What? I don't know. Nothing good," Terri said, yawning and stretching. She continued, "The bank forecloses. Herman's homeless. I lose the sale—probably my job." Terri paused for another yawn. "Then I end up working at Walgreens selling Lola generic gin? I'm not psychic. I'm not even all that intuitive."

CHAPTER 27

TERRI WAS WALKING home from the police station. She was worried about Lola May, Mrs. Irish, and Herman, even though Eric "Ichabod" Greenfield assured her they were all unharmed in last night's events. The attorney told them he hadn't seen Mrs. May or Herman himself, but Mrs. Irish assured him Mrs. May was resting comfortably and Herman had picked up his weekly provisions from the back porch as usual. Terri had grown quite fond of young Storky and hoped she never had a reason to see him again. And, despite his assurances, Terri wanted to see Lola and Herm and Mrs. Irish for herself. But they'd kept her hostage at the police station forever. Terri was too shattered to do anything but go home and fling herself into bed.

Then E. Shay drove up beside her. He rolled his window down.

"Get in."

It was like getting hit by lightning. Terri's energy instantly shot up. Shitty as he'd treated her in the police station, her traitorous heart still did a little flip when he was near.

"My choices were Mrs. Vaughn or walk," Terri said in an effort to sound less eager when she got in the car. Damn, he looked good to her. There was a palpable current running between them—a chemical connection so strong Terri couldn't understand how he didn't feel it too.

"I'll drive you home," E. Shay said. *Ooh, maybe he did feel it?* Terri thought. *Or maybe he drives everyone home from his interrogations.*

"Thanks. I guess you were just doing your job in there," Terri said, adding, "You make a fabulous bastard." A small laugh escaped Shay. Terri was encouraged. She kept going. "And showing up at the police station doesn't count if you've brought me there yourself. Which technically, you did."

E. Shay answered her gravely. "Yes. It does. What do you want me to say? I think you're in serious trouble, Terri."

"That's still better than saying—" She thought about it a second, "Who's Terri?"

Shay tried so hard not to laugh. He really did, but a snort escaped him. They arrived at Terri's building, and E. Shay parked illegally in front. He turned off the ignition.

"May I come up?" he asked to Terri's total delight.

****

Inside Terri's freight elevator, E. Shay cleared his throat nervously. *That's so sweet,* Terri thought.

"Terri, you're a witness but also still a suspect in a criminal investigation."

"I know. It's so preposterous. But good. Right? I mean, here we are," Terri said brightly. "I'm nervous too, can you tell? I'm talking, and I can't shut up." *Why did you say that?* Terri dissed herself. *You're making everything awkward and weird. Just shut up.*

The doors to Terri's elevator clanked open and Terri and E. Shay stepped out into her apartment. As she promised herself, Terri didn't say a word. The late afternoon sun scorched her loft with pink and tangerine light. They stood together in a golden halo. E. Shay could hardly take in the mad jumble before him. It was chaotic, yet wonderful. There was art everywhere—layers of it in all mediums. E. Shay marveled at the tapestry wall hung with mirrors and paintings, the life-sized carousel horse standing beside a decoupage mounting block, and a fantastic dirigible dangling from the exposed steel beams overhead.

E. Shay walked further inside the loft and turned around in a super-slow-motion circle. Then he stopped. He was facing the portrait of himself on the easel by the door.

"Whoa." E. Shay actually shouted.

Whoa, is right. Terri thought. *Shit. How could I have forgotten that was there?*

Terri lunged in front of the portrait like Joey Bosa on defense. "No, don't look at that. Shit. I'm—I'm a stalker." she declared. E. Shay walked forward. He bodily picked Terri up and moved her out of the way so he could see the portrait more clearly.

"How many portraits of me do you have?" he asked.

"One. No. Two. But one's on the back of my electric bill."

"What are these spots?" E. Shay wanted to know and moved right up close to the painting. "Christ, you gave me acne?" He said, incredulous, and then howled with laughter. He couldn't stop. He was tearing up he laughed so hard. And then they were both laughing. And then, somehow, they were kissing and laughing. Then they were just kissing. Then really, really kissing. Star-spangled kissing. Preexhausting, jungle-sex kissing that ends with a heap of sweaty and rumpled clothes on the floor.

****

They had the exhausting jungle sex. Thrice. But E. Shay prevented the rumples. He had folded Terri's clothes and his own, and placed them neatly on top of a magazine and book-littered table. It was an hour before dawn, and E. Shay lay awake beside Terri, silently berating himself. He couldn't believe he'd slept with her. Three times. And in the middle of a case. *Dumb. Big dumb.* How would he make his exit now? He wasn't good at playing the coward, but wasn't discretion the better part of valor? *Just go, Shay,* he told himself.

E. Shay crept carefully out of bed, practically holding his breath and dressed as silently as he could in the dark, trying not to disturb Terri. But he did. She heard enough to struggle awake—at her usual snail-like speed.

"Hi—wow," Terri said with a groggy smile.

"Hey," he said. E. Shay wasn't returning Terri's grin. "I have to go," he said. He picked up Terri's folded clothes from the night before.

"Okay. Thanks for the ride—and for the ride," she said, striving for humor and nonchalance. Not easy considering she'd just had the most outstanding sex of her life. She gave him another drowsy grin. "And for folding those. That's very sweet."

Yikes. I think I'm in love with him.

"You're welcome. But I need to take these. Your shoes too," E. Shay said. "For the lab." That woke Terri up.

"What?" she leapt up, naked and incredulous.

"I need the clothes and shoes you wore yesterday. For the lab. It's why I asked to come in. I told you. You're still a witness. Possibly a suspect." Shay spoke with a deliberate calm that was infuriating in and of itself.

"I have to rule you out, Terri." E. Shay placated. "You and Mrs. Vaughn both. Another officer went to collect her things." *My God.*

Didn't she know she was standing there, stark naked, and all E. Shay wanted to do was jump on her?

My God. Didn't he know if he kept standing there she was going to shoot him with his own gun? Terri was in a mounting rage, too furious for speech. But she had excellent aim. She hurled the shoes in question at E. Shay's head, followed by whatever else she could reach. Shay caught the shoes in self-defense and left as fast as he could.

****

E. Shay hadn't made a mistake of this magnitude in a long time. Sleeping with Terri had made everything worse. Now he was completely besotted with her and wantonly compromising an investigation. He knew he should have collected her things last night and brought them to the lab right then. But she was irresistible. And it wasn't a chain of evidence situation.

Or so he kept telling himself.

Her footprints and Vanessa's were only needed to compare to any strange footprints possibly left by the killer. Same with their clothing. Fibers found at the crime scene that didn't belong to Terri or Vanessa may be from the murderer's clothes. God willing, they'd find some of both. Regardless, E. Shay knew better. He'll be lucky not to get fired. He needed therapy.

Something was wrong with him.

Terri electrocuted someone. Terri was at the May Estate all the time. Terri was at the detention center. Terri knew the deceased. *Until Terri, nothing like this had ever happened before. To any of us*, E. Shay thought. And true to form, he'd fallen in love with her. A psycho.

Shay's radio squawked. An erratically driving vehicle was sighted on Gun Club Road near Interstate 95. He swung his car around and hit the gas hard. He'd already convinced himself the lab could wait. Instead, E. Shay would literally drive Terri out of his mind for the time it took him to catch up with these offenders. He turned on his arsenal of flashing lights and the siren.

In an apparent escape attempt, the boxy, over-sized truck E. Shay chased drove over the curb and up a steep embankment. It got stuck there with its front wheels spinning air like a turtle on its shell. Two men jumped from the truck's cab and ran off in different directions. *Guess something's up,* E. Shay concluded. He pulled over to the side of the road and parked. He jogged up the embankment to the truck and checked the cab. There was nothing inside but fast food wrappers. The truck was dirty. It had ghost lettering on its sides from a previous operator that read: "Lantana Glass Supply." Shay walked around back and saw it had no license plate.

The doors were closed with a cheap lock. E. Shay pulled out his key chain, found the small tool he needed, and picked the lock. E. Shay swung open the truck's back doors and was assaulted with a scent so putrid he dropped to his knees and became reflexively sick. He slammed the trucks back doors closed and ran to his car, taking deep breaths to calm his gag reflex. It was that bad. He dug out the gear he'd ordinarily use in a fire or toxic contamination situation, and he put it on. E. Shay returned to the truck. He opened the back again. The smell was inescapable.

The truck was filled with dead animals of all sizes stuffed into clear plastic bags. Printed on the sides of the bags were the words: "Property of Peaceful Pet Crematorium."

What the hell? E. Shay had really thought he'd seen everything in Baltimore. But he hadn't seen this.

CHAPTER 28

THE MAY ESTATE had been vandalized, and Lola May had not left her room since, nor could Herman be coaxed out of his shed. That left Terri, Mrs. Irish, and Joel to inventory the damage. It was everywhere. All the little lights Joel and Terri had painstakingly strung had been cut down and snarled beyond redemption. The canopy of petrified bougainvillea that made such a convincing veranda was crushed and broken and hanging over the house like a shroud. Joel's gorgeous fountain of flowers was a ruin of petals, pottery shards, and dirt. The staked-off terraced room had been obliterated, and Lola's dining room chairs had been thrown in the pool. The back lawn looked like it had been blow-torched.

Inside, the floor was covered with sand. There were holes punched in the walls and broken chandelier crystals on the floor. The foyer and hall were stained with spray paint. The drapery had been ripped down and shredded. And so had Terri's watercolor series: all six of them.

They weren't that *terrible*, she thought. Joel tried to prevent Terri from becoming completely demoralized.

"It's not that bad. I have a vision. I can see it," Joel said.

"Can you see it by Tuesday?" Terri said. It was a monumental clean-up task before them, and they both knew it. Thank goodness the vandals had ignored the tent. The tent just became the single most important selling feature May Estate had. Lola's house looked like an Italian army barracks once again.

"When do you think Herman's going to come out of that shed?" Joel asked.

"Night?" Terri answered.

Angelo arrived in his big Mercedes. He strode inside and said, "Oh holy—What's happened here? I can't believe this. This is horrible. Just horrible. What have you done?"

"Me? I—Mrs. May's was vandalized." Terri stammered.

"This is a disaster. We have buyers coming next week." Angelo squeaked. "Next week."

"Someone was murdered here," Terri said.

"No. Murdered? Oh dear, we're talking about a stigmatized property. That will have to be disclosed. Unless it was on the beach, below the highwater mark. Was it, do you know?" Angelo asked. Terri was almost certain he was Angelo. It was Angelo's license plate.

"Ah no," Terri answered.

Angelo suddenly drew himself up and looked around like the murderer was still there lurking. He asked, suspicious, "I haven't heard anything about this on the news or in the papers. Why is that?"

Terri and Joel shrugged a "beats me." A large truck rumbled up the driveway, scraping both its sides on the encroaching jungle. Terri recognized it as from the Safari Company, and she walked over to meet it. They were the same crew who had installed the tent.

"Hey, guys. I don't know what you've heard but your tent's fine," Terri said.

"I haven't heard anything, but was served with this first thing this morning." The tent boss handed the paper to Terri. It was a violation report. The Safari Company's tent permit was hereby revoked. There would be a $1,000 fine imposed for each day the tent remained past receiving this notice. Terri did not sit down right there and sob. But she was close.

Terri called Molly about the situation.

"In all the years I've been doing this," Molly said, "I've never had one of my tent permits revoked. Not for a wedding or a rock concert or a county fair. Go back to the Permits Office. Tell them they screwed up."

Terri did as she was advised and was told there was no mistake. The permit had been revoked. "But why? By whom?" Terri wanted to know.

"Someone above me, sister," Rosella the permit clerk said. "They tell me. I do it. If I get the right paperwork, that is."

"Who's 'they?' And my paperwork was impeccable," Terri insisted. Rosella looked at Terri sympathetically.

"I can see that. I don't know why they pulled your permit. A tent's a tent far, as I can tell. If it were me? I'd try the Planning and Zoning Commission. Any one of them could sign off on it. The meeting's public, and you're in luck. They meet today."

****

This again, Terri thought, though this was a good deal meaner than the genteel, Historic Preservation and Landmarks Board meeting she'd petitioned in Palm Beach. The West Palm Beach Town Hall was large and loud. The Planning and Zoning Commissioners sat on a stage in metal folding chairs with water bottles by their feet. The room was room full of people who were all clamoring for the commissioners' attention, and the clerk laughed at Terri when she tried to get on today's docket.

They have to take breaks, Terri thought. *I'll convince one of them during the break. How hard can it be to get one signature?* She slunk to the back of the auditorium and sat down. She'd size these commissioners up—find herself an easy target. Commissioner Chinless, lackey Scotty Berens, was among them. Beside him was one of his wife's look-a-likes from the luncheon.

If he had an affair with her, how would he even know? Terri wondered.

There were four very elderly commissioners who didn't speak at all and simply followed where Scotty Berens led. That left a bosomy, fifty-something Terri named Mrs. Robinson. She, at least, expressed some rational opinions along with a ton of cleavage. Terri had nearly decided on Mrs. Robinson as her target until Mrs. Robinson began giggling and flirting with Scotty instead of defending her own completely valid point. Then she acquiesced meekly when Commissioner Scotty dismissed her out of hand.

That left only Carlton: sixty-six-years old, wearing a plaid blazer with a comb-over hairdo. His skin was hairless and looked damp, like a baby's. He was Carlton Dowd Melon Smith III, born and raised in Palm Beach to its second-most affluent family. He'd been a Palm Beach town or county commissioner since he was eighteen-years-old, so he could sway the vote whenever he was needed. Carlton was as close to a moron as a person could be without a medical designation. Besides Carlton, there were six other absent commissioners.

Do something. Terri commanded herself. *You've got one option. One. Get in the game, you twit.* Terri took a breath and snuck from her seat in the back to the very foot of the stage. In a half-crouch, she edged her way toward the stage stairs. *Come on, already.*

Her thighs were shaking from her half-crouched position. She didn't want to block the views behind her. Ten eternal minutes later, the commissioners took a break. *To hell with strategy*, Terri thought. *I'll take whomever I can get.*

It was crazy how much the first woman off the stage looked like Linda Berens. She could have been the commissioner's wife's doppelganger. Or her twin.

"Excuse me? Hi. I'm Terri? We met at the Historic Preservation and Landmarks Society luncheon. And—I absolutely love your hair?" Terri finished lamely, lying through her teeth.

"Thank you." enthused the Twin Linda. "We all go to Jean Michelle. He's the best, but he rarely takes new clients." She gave Terri the once over. "Still, you can try. He could refer you to his protégés, I suppose."

Terri shamelessly followed Twin Linda into the ladies' room, and when Twin Linda was trapped peeing in the loo, delivered an extemporaneous plea, no doubt inspired by their surroundings. "The tent is more than practical. It's—it's antiseptic. As a realtor, I see the kinds of people shopping for houses," Terri said this in a tone that suggested Terri saw lepers shopping for houses, but she was envisioning her fellow realtors. "Some of them I can't even describe."

But some I could. Like June Alice the egg-shaped, social-climbing toady. "Would you, or anyone, want to buy a house where hundreds of people had used the facilities? Of course not. Bathrooms are simply too personal," Terri said.

FLUSH.

"Yes. I hadn't thought of that," Twin Linda conceded, coming out of the stall.

"Every home on the market in Palm Beach could be sullied. All because of some glitch," Terri said and handed the woman a paper towel. "But no harm, no foul." Terri kept following the duplicate commissioner's wife all the way back to the auditorium. "You can sign this and the Pee-Pee tent is back up, just like that." Terri SNAPPED her fingers for emphasis. She held out the tent permit in one hand and a pen in the other.

"Oh. Yes, I suppose. It's much more sanitary isn't it?" Twin Linda took Terri's offered pen and then suddenly, out of nowhere, Carlton lunged forward and grabbed Twin Linda's extended arm with both his damp and hairless paws. The blonde, bird-like Twin Linda winced in pain.

"Has there been a motion? I didn't hear any motion. We don't sign anything without a motion. Who made a motion?" Carlton was shouting and becoming increasingly agitated and unhinged. Twin Linda tried to wriggle out of Carlton's grasp but couldn't. Her hand was turning blue. Commissioner Scotty strode over and took charge. He took Carlton literally under-wing and unhanded his wife's duplicate.

"No. No motions, Carlton, you're entirely right," Scotty said soothingly before asking, "What are we signing?" like he was an actor in a play.

"A tent permit," Terri said. "It was granted and mistakenly revoked. It's nothing. I only need a signature."

"Wait. There may be more here. A moment," Scotty said, all concerned, and winked at Terri.

Uck. He rallied his returning commissioners around him with a gesture that made his chin disappear entirely. The commissioners congregated around Scotty at the steps to the stage. Scotty kept his wife's twin close by his side. Terri couldn't hear what was said, but she could see the commissioners' shocked and animated faces. What was going on? Since when is a tent permit shocking?

After another two minutes of conferring, Scotty motioned for Terri to join the clump of commissioners before they resumed being seated on stage. He spoke to her in a confidential whisper, loud enough for everyone to hear.

"There have been, in other parts of the state, several issues with gypsy campgrounds." The gathered commissioners nodded solemnly in agreement.

"Gypsy campgrounds? Are you kidding me?" Terri asked before she could censor herself.

"The huge problem with guns and alcohol. The opioid crisis. We had to respond." *What is he talking about?* Terri thought. "New legislation cracked down on all temporary shelters, like gypsy caravans. A lot of illegal immigration happens that way. Your tent got caught up in the dragnet. Please, understand it happens sometimes. But we're all patriots here, right? Am I right?"

Scotty asked his fellow commissioners, who agreed wholeheartedly, even those who'd just arrived and didn't know what was going on. Scotty squeezed Terri's hand, like that settled everything. He bounded onto the stage, towing a stupidly preening Carlton. The rest of the commissioners followed him and took their seats.

CHAPTER 29

TERRI DIDN'T KNOW what to expect, but it wasn't this. She inched her car up Ursula and Ben Lurie's beautifully landscaped driveway, as slowly as she could, and arrived at an astounding, white mansion. Terri was shocked. Unlike Ursula and Ben, this place reeked of excellent taste. The large and beautiful house was set on an even larger, manicured lawn. It was grand, yet restrained. It was scrupulously symmetrical and elegant. Terri only wanted to sit there absorbing the brilliance of its architecture and the graciousness of its proportions; however, as soon as she stopped her car, Ursula all but dragged Terri out of it.

She had taken Terri by the hand. *By the hand.* And now Ursula was towing Terri across the length of their expansive, limestone living room floor at a trot. Without stopping, pausing, or turning around, Ursula hauled Terri straight out the back doors to a stunning covered loggia area, where they were greeted with another acre of manicured, emerald lawn. Except for two exquisite fountains, the lawn rolled unimpeded to the intercoastal waterway. An eighty-foot yacht was tied at the Lurie's dock.

"If you do not include ze rooms for ze servants, there are seven bedrooms with ze bath. The spa, his and hers, yes? You go from zee master suite. From zee cabana both." Ursula's narration had gotten more breathless by the room.

She had hustled Terri up and down four sets of stairs and in and out of twelve-and-a-half-thousand square feet of mansion, like they were running a 5K race. Off of the loggia, Ursula opened another door to an opulent cabana bathroom.

"Zo you zee whole of house now," Ursula said, breathlessly.

"Yes. And weren't you efficient," Terri said, bent over, hands on her knees, trying to catch her own breath. Terri checked her watch. "Damn, Ursula. You're good. I mean Mrs. Lurie. Eleven minutes flat. You should be in real estate." Terri stopped for another breath. "It's not even three o'clock. I guess that's when your next appointment is?"

"Every fuckin' day." Ben Lurie shouted.

"Don't say," Ursula scolded her ancient husband, who had shuffled in from some other part of the house—presumably their bedroom. He wore a bathrobe and slippers.

"Why not?" Ben wanted to know. "Ain't that the reason she's here, for Christ's sakes." He shouted at his young and enhanced wife.

"I am telling this." Ursula shouted right back. "Ve vant for you to sell zee house." She turned to Terri, still shouting.

Am I having a daylight hallucination? Terri wondered. *OK, Just feeling faint from the tour, or am I being punked or pranked or whatever it's called these days?* Terri looked around. Was a camera crew going to jump out of the trees?

"Uh—um, Mr. and Mrs. Lurie? I, we, looked at townhouses and condominiums for two weeks. Two weeks. You and you and me, remember? Tami? Then you locked me out on a balcony—to die?" *Shit. Maybe they are trying to kill me?* "Does that ring any bells?"

"You vill sell our house." Ursula barked with such ferocity her German ancestors would have been proud. They probably heard her.

"Okay. I'll do it. I'll sell your house." Terri quickly agreed.

Thinking, *This is surreal. And am I having a stroke?* She put her hands on her cheeks to feel them moving symmetrically. Terri alarmed herself further, stuttering, "Um, this is probably a f-forty million dollar property." Listings like this did not happen to agents like Terri. *I concede, horse-faced Title woman. You had a point.*

"I'll take fifteen." Ben snarled. *Fifteen?* Ben looked at his watch and said, "Wait for it."

Fifteen?

Then Ursula flung herself face down on a lounge chair, sobbing. *Whoa. What is going on here?* This was real distress. Terri could tell. Ursula hadn't arranged herself at all attractively. She had sprawled across the divan with her dress twisted up in an unfortunate, cellulite exposing way. She whimpered into her silk upholstery.

Meanwhile, Ben casually offered Terri a cigar. "Ya sure? Ya sure now?" Terri was sure. When she declined the third time, Ben said, "Don't say I didn't offer." Ben unwrapped his cigar, clipped the end, and struck a match to it. Between puffs, he counted down with great ceremony.

"Four." Puff in. Puff out. "Three." In. Out. "Two." Big puff in and long, long stream of smoke later, "One."

A shadow blanketed the estate from west to east. Terri could feel the change in the air pressure. It was heavy and damp and the sky grew darker. A growing *whup, whup, whup,* sounded in Terri's ears, and the hairs on the back of her neck stood up. Moments later, hundreds of horrifying vultures landed all over Ursula and Ben Luries' formerly valuable estate. Hideous, ripe vultures, bigger than golden retrievers, stood lined up along the dock and on the upper decks of the boat. They stood on the giant flower urns, on bannisters, on balconies. They landed with thuds onto the roof and carpeted the lawn from dock to loggia.

"Holy shit." Terri blurted and covered her mouth with both hands.

"Ve do not know vat to do. Two years now, ve have been making zee house and having never a problem." Weeping made Ursula harder to understand, but Terri was getting the gist, despite being so skeeved out she was shaking with it.

"Then April. April-bloody-twenty-third. At three in the afternoon," Ben said. "They came. First in ones and twos. Then *fagedaboudit.*"

Terri said nothing. She was concentrating on breathing through her mouth. The stench was overwhelming. The giant, putrid creatures ventured even closer. She could see the pebbled skin draped around their upper bodies and necks—and the horrible red-pebbled gobble, draping from their mouths like so many entrails.

A few walked onto the patio where Terri, Ursula, and Ben Lurie stood. Where they stood. The smell made Terri's nose run. Oh, why did she refuse that cigar? Terri had instinctively moved beside the doors into the house.

"Shouldn't we go inside?" Terri asked, just wanting to get the fuck out of there. But Ursula was determined to explain.

"Ve do ze extermination for months and months and months. Iz okay. Zen comes zee notice ve must stop. And now ve must stop, poof, no more, for zee environmentalism, yes?"

What? Terri lost the plot. Though she was sitting up, Ursula held a silk pillow (no doubt heavily scented) over her mouth and nose, making it extra hard to understand her.

Then Ben shouted, "The property's a Goddamn vulture hatchuary. Do you believe that? Who the hell's ever heard of a vulture hatchuary?" Ben demanded. *Not me,* Terri thought, near tears. She wanted to throw up. "Goddamn protected vulture hatchuary." Ben repeated.

Ursula dropped her pillow and gripped both of Terri's hands hard, like she was going to make Terri take a blood oath.

"You vill sell ze house before everyone iz to know, yes? Othervise, ve lose all."

Alright already, Terri thought. God knew almost nothing put a buyer off a property like nesting vultures.

"Um, how long do they stay here for?" Terri asked, trying not to gag.

"All night. But iz not zo bad. In ze dark, ze look like ze flamingos, yes?"

"If you're blind." *Shit.* Terri hadn't meant to say that out loud.

"Ya see. Ya see, Ursey. I told ya." Ben lit into Ursula. Terri just wanted to get inside the house and away from these vultures.

Vultures. Terri's skin was crawling off her body. *Why couldn't this have been a nice, normal meth lab?*

CHAPTER 30

"GYPSIES? WHAT A BUNCH of rot," Joel said after hearing Terri's tale about the tent permit. The luxury bedroom tents could not be part of the May Estate sales equation anymore. Lola May's meager 3,000-square-foot home was all there was. The upstairs would have to be reconverted back into bedrooms. The pending 1,800-square-foot terraced room and Lola's priceless columns were the only exploitable assets left and took on a much greater significance in the sale. The bottom line was May Estate owed the Whitney Bank $16 million. No one made a dime before that debt was paid.

If it was paid.

Thank God Lola May's insurance was up to date. Terri called in every favor she had with painters, landscapers, and the crime scene cleaners she'd used repeatedly since the infamous meth house. She'd cajoled, bribed, and flirted like the desperado she was and had gotten all of them there within a day. Terri would be painting baby and pet portraits for the rest of her natural life.

Now, even cleaned and freshly painted, Lola May's house looked small and bare to Terri. But she was prepared to make the case for pristine, elegant, and understated. Unadorned, with not so much as a twig for decoration, the arched and paned windows stood out nicely in stark relief. A much wider perimeter around the whole house had been cleared and laid with fresh sod. And the fountain had been resurrected with gorilla glue and duct tape. Joel stuffed it with green cascading ivy. It wasn't terrible.

Now they only had to make Lola May's house look appealing inside, like it was in Palm Beach, not Kandahar. Joel had convinced Terri that the least expensive, quickest way to fluff up Lola's house was to raid Terri's art collection and cover the damage with it. Before Terri could refuse him, Joel had loaded up the elevator and was gone with a mouthy, "See ya."

For one sickening moment, Terri thought it was a Timothy scam all over again, which left her breathless. It threw her, and she couldn't shake a sick sense of foreboding from clinging through the afternoon. Terri stood forlornly in Lola's foyer with Joel and Mrs. Irish.

"Right here at the foot of the stairs needs something lovely. Oh, this be lovely, isn't it?" Mrs. Irish said. She was looking through a stack of paintings leaning against the wall.

"And it's just the right size too," Mrs. Irish added, carefully lifting it up. It was the painting of the Spanish castle house Terri watched get towed up the intracoastal waterway while she was trapped on the balcony. Up the River Without a Paddle was just big enough to cover all three holes in the wall at the foot of Lola's front stairs.

Joel picked up the next painting in the stack leaning against the wall. It was the portrait of E. Shay. "Oh, honey, you are good," Joel said. "Tell me he's not your imagination."

"He's not," Terri said.

"He simply must be hung," Joel said.

"He deserves to be hung," Terri replied.

"Ah-oh. Do you want to tell Auntie Joel about it? Is it love-hate or hate-hate?" Joel tried to jolly Terri out of her funk. They had been working in a silent fugue for a while. Terri finally stopped working and stepped back to reassess the situation. She saw the interior was rapidly shaping up. It wasn't nearly what they'd achieved before, but it was appealing. And crisp. When in doubt, fresh white paint was Joel's mantra. *Maybe all wasn't lost,* Terri told herself. Now wasn't the time to give up. Now was the time to take a short, bolstering Titos's break. *Yes? Yes, it was totally that time.*

Terri told Mrs. Irish, "Joel and I are going out for half an hour. Do you or Lola need anything?"

"We're all good, lovey," Mrs. Irish said, and Terri and Joel left.

CHAPTER 31

THEY'D JUST CLOSED the front door behind them when Terri and Joel saw a familiar big, black Mercedes roll up to the front of Mrs. May's house and stop. Angelo got out of the driver's side. His license plate read "PPPAng." Anthony's read "PPPAnt." June Alice climbed out of the passenger side and carried a fake Louis Viton purse to match her fake Louis Viton portfolio.

"Hi, Angelo. We're not ready yet. But we're very close. *So* close," Terri said, mustering enthusiasm. Angelo and June Alice slammed their doors.

"Your license has been revoked." Angelo barked. *What?* Terri was speechless. Joel's mouth dropped open. Angelo continued, "Debeeper." he said furiously. It's hard to say debeeper—DBPR or the Department of Business and Professional Relations—seriously, let alone furiously. Terri and Joel suppressed grins.

"The Florida Real Estate Commission has revoked your real estate license. They've threatened to close Premium Property Partners down for employing you."

"I'm not technically an employee," Terri said. "I'm an independent contractor."

"Then for contracting you. Do you know how this makes us look? Having a criminal for a sales agent?" Angelo demanded.

"I'm not a real criminal," Terri protested.

"You're on probation, aren't you? At the Everglades Rehabilitation and Detention Center? Are you going to deny it?" Terri was a deer in the headlights under Angelo's assault. She had never seen him this angry before. How could all this have gotten so out of hand? Terri was only trying to do her best for her clients.

A big gas guzzling Range Rover pulled up behind Angelo's Mercedes, and Brinker Deeley climbed out with a grunt.

He flicked his hair back and went straight over to Angelo, as if Terri weren't standing beside him. Brinker had brought the original low offer for the May Estate with him, and he handed it to Angelo.

"You must be Brinker Deeley. You're right on time. Angelo Virga. So nice meeting you. I'd like you to meet June Alice. One of our associates at Premium Property Partners. Mrs. May is more comfortable with a woman handling her affairs. That's why I've brought June Alice along to tender your offer."

"I'm really looking forward to working with you, Mr. Deeley," June Alice gushed.

"Fine. Can we get on with it?" Brinker said boorishly and flicked his hair back again.

"My pleasure," Angelo said, holding the front door open for Brinker and June Alice to precede him into the house. Angelo turned back to Terri.

"I want you and whatever you've brought in here that doesn't belong to Mrs. May off the property within the hour." Angelo shut Lola's front door behind him.

Terri and Joel sat down together on Lola's front step.

"This is so wrong. Terri, I'm sorry," Joel consoled her. They sat together in silence for another five minutes.

"One of us, who's not me, has to function." Terri said.

Joel gave her a kiss on the head, stood up, and went inside. He'd start taking down everything they'd just finished putting up. *Poor Terri.* She'd killed herself on this listing and was depending on it in more ways than just climbing out of the financial hole her shitty ex-husband, Tim, had put her in.

Terri sat on Lola's stoop, thinking exactly that. *Why am I still such a twit? Everything I touch turns to crap. Now I don't even have a real estate license. How humiliating. A real estate license. That's like having a beautician's license revoked. You only had to be conscious to qualify for a real estate license. Mine's revoked.*

Terri was having quite the pity party. She sat on Lola May's front step and sniveled and sniffed and cursed. She was so engrossed with feeling sorry for herself that she didn't hear Herman creep up silently beside her.

"Herm." she shrieked. "Jesus, Herm, you scared the cheese out of me." Herman handed Terri a bouquet of exotic flowers he had harvested from the deeper reaches of Lola May's property: hibiscus, jasmine, and a huge bird of paradise—all crushed together in a slightly mangled bunch. Terri cried harder. He put them down on the steps before her and lumbered away in his uneven gate with his head bowed. "Oh, Herman. You are a wonderful, sweet man," Terri said. She picked up the bouquet and held the flowers to her tear-streaked face. She smiled sadly and sniffed deeply. A beetle the size of a lobster crawled onto her face.

"*Aaaaaah.*" Terri flung the bouquet as far as she could and dashed inside, slamming Lola's door behind her.

CHAPTER 32

CAN NOTHING GO right? Terri stood up in front her painting, Up the River Without a Paddle. She tried to collect herself. Her usual humor and optimism seemed to have deserted her just when she needed them most. *I'm thinking in country music clichés,* Terri thought, a little hysterically. She now understood wanting to scream—scream until she fainted from hypoxia. But she wouldn't. Not here. At least, she didn't think so. And, of course, Vanessa Vaughn was right on que. Terri could smell her Chanel No. 5 perfume from the top of the stairs. *Yep, here she is.*

"Terri. I was just up with Lola May. Now you're going to have to—"

And Terri snapped. Just like that. She cut Vanessa off mid-word and lost it. All Terri's built-up frustration came rushing to the surface in a torrential fury.

She snarled, "No. No, I don't Mrs. Vaughn. Whatever it is, I'm not doing it. I'm not putting up gates. I'm not electrocuting people. I'm not calling God the Baby Jesus Christ our Savior. I'm not identifying dead bodies. I'm not painting weasels. And I'm not practicing real estate. Not anymore." Terri turned back to her painting and would have torn it off the wall, but it was nailed up there. By then, Vanessa had descended the stairs and stood beside Terri.

"Tsk. What an odd picture," Vanessa said. "Beautiful, don't get me wrong. How could it not be? *Casa Rosa* is an iconic Palm Beach land-mark, hmm? But to paint it without its roses? Ridiculous. It's named House of Roses. The artist must be a fool."

"There were no roses," Terri bit out.

"There are always roses at *Casa Rosa*. The gardeners orchestrate different species to bloom year round, dear. I know. I was on the Historic Preservation Society Board when *Casa Rosa* was originally landmarked. It's the most enchanting scene. Right at the end of Pe-ruvian Lane. Why are you looking at me in that most peculiar way?"

Terri took Vanessa by the arm and all but carried her outside to her car. She strapped Vanessa in and took off in a spray of gravel. Vanessa, being Vanessa, objected and fought Terri the whole way. "What are you doing? Unhand me." Vanessa protested. "I don't want to get in your grubby little car."

"Too bad," Terri said, silently praying Vanessa would just shut up until they got there. Terri drove like a demon, but Vanessa never stopped talking.

"I don't know where this is coming from, Terri. But these out-bursts of yours are beginning to get out of hand, hmm? I won't always be around to tell you when to pull yourself together, you know?"

"No, I didn't know. But I hoped and prayed," Terri said and turned her car abruptly onto Peruvian Lane and then came to a screeching stop in front of *Casa Rosa*. More accurately in front of an eighteen-foot-high wire fence covered by a wall of fake ivy. The backdrop for a billboard-sized rendering of the future *Casa Rosa Villas*—an ex-clusive waterfront community of ultraluxury, concierge villas—from the $6 millions.

"Dear. You ha—" Vanessa stopped short when they'd climbed out of the car. Terri hadn't known what to expect either, but she could have guessed. This wasn't even subtle. They walked up to the fake hedge fence and smooshed their faces between the gaps to see what was behind it. There were the remains of a huge swimming pool with beautiful Moroccan tiling. It was half excavated. The foundation of the house was still clear. It was the footprint of the house Terri had painted. Used to be anyway. Vanessa was having palpitations. "This can't be."

"Is," Terri said.

"You don't seem to understand, dear. This can't be. You can't tear down a landmark. That's what land-marking prevents."

"Maybe it was infested?"

"It was stone. It's made of stone. This shouldn't be. *Casa Rosa* is an important part of Palm Beach history. This is a travesty."

Terri was looking at the billboard rendering. It looked like an office park. A giant concrete and glass building surrounded by rose bushes. Terri mentally whacked up the six-story structure and did the math. "Holy shit." Terri said. Her thoughts racing. "Those bastards."

"What bastards? Who? Are you listening to me?" Vanessa said, but Terri was already halfway back to her car. Vanessa scurried to keep up with Terri and quickly got in Terri's passenger side. Terri had dragged a bunch of printouts from the chaos in her back seat onto her lap in the driver's seat and was looking for something.

"It's here somewhere," Terri said, and then seemed to find what she sought. "Oh my God, oh my God, oh my God."

"Please stop saying that, Terri. Aren't you an atheist or something?" Vanessa said.

"What? No. Maybe? Mrs. Vaughn—buckle up," Terri said and peeled out.

CHAPTER 33

BRINKER DEELEY WAS in a temper before he'd arrived at Lola May's and was not mollified when he got there. To him, Lola May's hadn't recovered at all from being vandalized.

Damn his uncle. He'd fought the judge bitterly over this arguing spraying graffiti around was enough. But not for the judge, even though he'd promised Brinker there'd be no more damage than paint and powder could fix. But Brinker saw expensive, custom windows had been broken too and valuable antique chairs were thrown in the pool. Brinker was working himself into quite the snit.

He strode from barren room to barren room like he already owned the place. He made note of everything that was missing from the preview reception and tried to figure out an addendum to get it all back, like those thrones at the head of Lola May's dining room table. Brinker wanted them. And the table. He wanted the tents too. Brinker coveted every curated piece Joel had artfully placed there for the reception. And, by God, he wanted it all back the way it was.

Brinker roamed out the backdoors for a look around, noticing the dramatic effect cutting all the landscape back had had on Lola May's house. When he returned inside it was extremely bright because the obscuring vines were entirely gone. Objectively, you'd never know it had been recently trashed. And it was finally occurring to Brinker that he'd better wrap this up before another agent turned up here with a much higher offer.

Brinker flicked his hair and climbed Lola's front hall stairs. He found everyone congregated outside of Lola May's door.

Mrs. Irish stood with her fists angrily on her hips. June Alice was on her knees feeding the contract, page by page, under Lola's door. Angelo stood over her looking deeply concerned.

"Please sign it in all the places marked X. There are eleven pages—" June Alice said, then turned to Angelo and Brinker. "If you want my opinion, she's gone to sleep."

"We don't. Explain it to her again. Plainly. So she understands there's no other choice," Brinker said.

June Alice spoke facing under the door. "Mrs. May, you have to sell your house. Do you want the bank to foreclose and get nothing? You can't keep this house. You may as well get used to living in reduced circumstance."

Mrs. Irish did not like that remark. "Who do you be thinking you are, you feckless slag?" she said before rounding on Angelo and Brinker and suggesting they all go away.

"Are you the maid?" Brinker said to Mrs. Irish. "Do you want to be responsible for Mrs. May losing everything she owns?"

"I've been telling you, Mrs. May won't be coming out again until late this eve, you daft man." Mrs. Irish said.

June Alice couldn't wait to add, "This offer doesn't expire until noon tomorrow. That's what it says on the contract." June Alice was delighted with herself.

Brinker could have strangled her. *Shut up, you dumb cow.* Brinker thought meanly, flicked his hair, and said, "The reason this deal isn't signed already is because you people are unprofessional hacks."

"That was uncalled for," Angelo said, then immediately apologized for all the imaginary delays and inconveniences Brinker had suppos-edly suffered. Angelo asked Mrs. Irish to please make them all tea, and Mrs. Irish said they hadn't got any.

"When I come back this contract had better be signed," Brinker said in a huff and lumbered down the stairs to come face to face with Terri's painting, Up the River Without a Paddle. He staggered back as if struck.

"Where did this painting come from?" Brinker wanted to know. June Alice and Angelo had followed Brinker down stairs.

"That's Terri's. Another realtor who used to work here. She's a criminal now. I never liked her," June Alice said.

Brinker growled something profane and strode out the front door.

CHAPTER 34

TERRI SHOULDN'T HAVE been amazed by Vanessa's monologue, but she was. Vanessa pontificated from the time they left *Casa Rosa Villa's* construction site until they arrived at the detention center. Vanessa orated through miles of white-knuckled speeds and teeth-shattering pot holes. Vanessa even talked through Terri's leaving the car in the detention center parking lot and running in for directions. Vanessa was mid-sentence when Terri returned.

She flung an open map in Vanessa's lap and peeled out of the detention center's parking lot. Within minutes the roads had deteriorated into little more than dirt tracks, winding through scrub and swamp. Terri interrupted, "Look for a sign that says: 'Drainage Canal 4-73.' It's little and green. It might just say '4-73.'"

"I'm not at all certain we should be doing this," Vanessa said and launched into another boorish speech.

It was okay. The farther they drove, the less irritating Vanessa was. God knew Terri never wanted to drive out here again. She just wanted to see for herself. And it never hurt to have a witness.

****

Herman's shed was larger than it looked on the inside. It was a two-storied structure with a substory where Herman bathed and slept. Shay and Herman sat across from each other on the ground floor of the only room with a box of assorted Duncan Donuts Shay had brought between them. E. Shay couldn't tell if Herman understood his questions or not.

"Do people come here during the night in boats, Herman? Have you seen boats close in here? Or on your beach?" E. Shay asked.

"Probably so," Herman answered and reached for his sixth donut.

"When Herman? Last month? Was the moon big? Or a little moon?" Shay asked.

"Probably not," Herman said.

Shit. E. Shay wasn't getting anywhere. He wanted some drug lords to be turfing each other out and this was their drop. He wanted Homeland Security to be foiling some attack from South America. Shay wanted it to be anything but Terri being a murderous, vandalizing psycho. But he needed to speak to her, and he couldn't find her anywhere. Not that he could blame her for avoiding him. Leaving as he did. With her clothes.

Herman was down to three glazed donuts and E. Shay was out of questions. He reviewed all of Herman's answers: "Probably so. Probably so. Probably not. And nighttime. Shay put his notepad away and stood up as best he could in the five-and-a-half-foot ceilinged room.

"Thank you, Herman. You don't happen to know where Terri is, do you?" E. Shay asked. At Terri's name, Herman made a horrible face. It took a moment for Shay to realize this was Herman's happy face. "Do you know where Terri is?" E. Shay repeated.

"Terri," Herman said. He stood and wrapped his knuckles on the ceiling. E. Shay had to drop down to his knees to look up at the shed's ceiling. Terri had painted the cow jumping over the moon nursery rhyme.

"You don't eat cats or dogs, do you? Nope, forget I asked."

CHAPTER 35

TERRI'S CAR WAS bouncing along at a spine-shattering speed. She did not want to be out here after dark. It was creepy enough in full daylight. And still Vanessa never stopped talking.

"And I'm extremely displeased that you've used my fondness for you to involve me in this, this, whatever it is. There it is." Vanessa said as Terri slammed on her brakes. They had been looking for another drainage canal sign. 48 C Drainage Canal. Terri turned onto an even bumpier trail.

"You're fond of me?" Terri asked.

"Don't be obtuse, though you do it well. Slow down, Terri. Now where to next?" Vanessa asked, even though she held the map and answered her own question. "Left across Drainage Canal 4-82. I assume there'll be another miniscule sign to search for? And it will be green, no doubt. What's the point of a sign if it's camouflaged, I ask you, hmm? And slow down. There."

Terri turned. Her car bounced wildly over a hard-packed, rutted road. The foliage was so thick around them that if they hadn't been looking hard they would have missed it. They definitely couldn't have found this place in the dark. The first thing they spotted was an old-time movie marquee: the kind with bulb lighting, though the bulbs were all broken. It stuck diagonally up from between the trees and advertised the movie *Love Story*, starring Ali McGraw and Ryan

O'Neil. As Terri drove farther in, they saw it was attached to an ancient, Baroque movie theater, covered in moss and set on a slant, like there'd been an earthquake. Or it had been put there without leveling the ground or pouring a foundation.

Terri drove slower. More crazily-tilted old buildings came into view, all in varying degrees of reclamation by Mother Nature. This was Everglades territory out here. Hot, low, swampy jungle. Super corrosive.

"Hey, Vanessa. Remember when you said you thought that hooker lived in a barn? And she said she lived in the past? And that flasher, he said, 'Yeah, the past was free?'" Terri asked.

"Yes. So? He wasn't a flasher, dear. I saw. He was wearing pants."

"They weren't talking about yesterday. They were talking about a place. Here. This place. This is the Past."

Terri crept along slowly. The farther they drove, the less overgrown the haphazardly strewn structures were. They passed half a dozen buildings before the road ended in front of *Casa Rosa*: the latest arrival to the Past. Like all the others, it had been left on unlevel ground, so it looked like it was sinking.

Terri got out of her car and went rummaging in her trunk. All her guilt for not cleaning out her car (or washing it) vanished. There was the rest of the printout from her petition research. She'd made Joel read it aloud to her on the way to that unfortunate dinner with his awful stepbrother. It listed every historic landmarked property in the county. And the tax rolls. It had printed out in teeny, tiny type, and Terri had given Joel her handy car magnifying glass to read it with.

"This really lives in your glove compartment?" Joel asked.

Terri replied, "I'm equipped. Magnifying glass, cocktail fork, corkscrew. You never know."

Vanessa had gotten out of Terri's car and walked to stand before *Casa Rosa*. She'd stopped talking.

This is worrisome, Terri thought. She stood beside Vanessa and read from her printout. "*Casa Rosa*. Historic landmark, built 1938. Last sale date: February 8, 2017, for $13,700,000." Terri stopped reading and said, "*Casa Rosa* is here. I'm looking at it. Right? I'm not imagining this? And back in town twenty-two *Casa Rosa Villas* are on sale for more than $132,000,000? Not a bad return on that investment. Gee, Vanessa, methinks someone has nefariously un-landmarked your landmark. And a bunch of other ones too." Vanessa still hadn't spoken. Her mouth was opening and closing but nothing was coming out. "Vanessa, do you recognize any of these other buildings?"

Terri led Vanessa to another vantage point where they could see through the trees more clearly. It was tough going. The ground was hard-packed and lumpy, like a thousand enormous tractor trailers had rolled through and left four-foot tire grooves. Shafts of sunlight lit up a billion dust motes, suspended in the thick, wet air, and the mosquitos were having a field day. Worse, it was ninety degrees outside.

"That one over there. Keeney Cottage. I remember I voted that down for landmarking. It had too many modifications, not enough qualifications. Hmm? And that must be, my God, the North Flagler Lending Library? *No.*" Vanessa cried.

What was left of the North Flagler Lending Library had partially crashed into Keeney Cottage. They were crunched together like they belonged to one building. Vanessa struggled farther along for a better view. From there, they estimated maybe as many as twenty buildings were in the Past. Houses, movie theater, library, and a courthouse. Just like a real town.

This is fucked up, Terri thought.

There were signs of habitation everywhere: clothes lines, rusty bicycles, some old dirty cars cursorily camouflaged. All of the dilapidated buildings had wires jerry-rigged haphazardly to their roofs and disappearing into the trees. They all had antennas.

Wow. If someone was trying to claim this was Section 8 housing, I'm a banana, Terri thought. *Could someone possibly be that brazen?*

It wasn't that expensive to cart these landmarks here when you consider the outrageous returns. And now that Terri'd thought about it, they were probably all floated here, like *Casa Rosa,* on a barge. There were a hundred tributaries leading into the Everglades. Especially when they had a water release from Lake Okeechobee.

BOOM. A crack of thunder sounded so loud both Terri and Vanessa jumped. It was instantly followed by a torrential downpour.

Shit, Terri thought. She'd wanted to take more pictures. And she really didn't want to ever come back here. They slipped and struggled their way back to Terri's car. Vanessa had lost a shoe, which had been sucked off in the rapidly deepening mud. It was slick beneath their feet and rivers were forming as high as their ankles before they reached the car. It poured buckets while they opened the doors and got in quickly. They were soaking wet. Half of Terri's research printout had bled and all but disintegrated. They sat in the car, drenched to their knickers, and the rain drowned out Vanessa's renewed orations. Terri could hardly believe how grateful she was Vanessa had started talking again. She turned her ignition on.

"What are you doing? You can't see a thing." Vanessa shouted the obvious at Terri, whose nose was glued to her windshield. The windshield wipers did nothing. Terri wanted them on higher ground lest they get stuck there. Her little car slowly bumped and slid and bounced its way up and down and hopped forward. The rain kept coming, and Terri stopped when she reached what felt like a slight elevation midway out of the Past. All four wheels were on the ground and the car was almost level. Terri's phone had no service, so she tuned Vanessa out and turned it to flashlight mode. Terri searched the remains of her printout.

"Keeney Cottage was landmarked in 2004," Terri said.

"That was the year I left the board," Vanessa said.

"Both Keeney Cottage and *Casa Rosa* were purchased in trust to Whitney Bank in 2005. The Whitney Bank foreclosed on them both in 2007 and 2009. Both were sold in 2015 for an undisclosed amount," Terri said.

"Dreadful people, those Whitneys. Not all of them, naturally, but Linda Berens and her sister Beth Deeley are Whitneys, and they're both insufferable, I can tell you. You'd think they were royalty for marrying a commissioner; plus the uncle is a judge," Vanessa elaborated.

A wave of understanding hit Terri. "Ahh. Thank you, Mrs. Vaughn. You just answered so many questions. Like, why those chicks all looked alike. Is the judge you mean Judge Montgomery, perhaps?"

"Of course, dear. He's the only judge who matters. Despicable as he is, he owns this county."

CHAPTER 36

JUDGE MONTGOMERY LISTENED with growing displeasure as Brinker detailed Up the River Without a Paddle for him. They were in Judge Montgomery's huge Bentley, driving west—fast. Unlike the ride in Terri's aging buggy, this ride was smooth and silent but for Brinker.

"*Casa Rosa* was perfectly detailed. There was a reflection of it in the water, so there were two of them. Couldn't have been more obvious it was being towed on a barge," Brinker said.

"You think this little realtor knows what's going on because of that? She doesn't know anything. Besides, we have a completely legitimate business operation out here," his wife, Beth Whitney Deeley, said from the back seat. "And she looks like a simpleton."

"Why couldn't we have just foreclosed like we did on those others? Now this bitch is going to ruin everything," Brinker whined. It was going to be his property after all. It was his due. Plus, he'd worked the hardest. All his wife had to do was void the fake mortgage on Lola May's house after he closed. How hard was that? *Push a delete button,* Brinker thought petulantly. He was the one on the front lines. He had to deal with that realtor disguising May's as bigger and more valuable than it was.

The judge's phone rang. It was his own personal Sheriff Jones out at the Everglades Rehabilitation and Detention Center: "Own" being the operative word. Jones confirmed Terri had been out at the center earlier in the day asking for directions to where the people who attended their mandatory service class might live. She was given directions out to Eleanora. That was the legal name for the Past on the County tax rolls. It was claimed as *Section 8* housing—with all the attendant tax breaks, even though it provided no electric, sewage, water, or safety services to the residents. Eleanora received additional subsidies as an historic village dedicated to restoration and preservation. The souls who squatted there, fearing deportation, prison, or worse were the judge's free personal labor pool. He liked having thugs on hand. And very young boys. The Past wasn't just the judge's personal playground either. It was a boon for everyone riding in Judge Montgomery's Bentley. This end of the operation more than paid for itself.

"We didn't think there was anything wrong with telling her," Sherriff Jones said, "Doubt she can find it. Most people don't their first try."

"Was she alone?" the judge asked, audibly unhappy.

"When she came in she was. But we think she had that old lady in the car with her."

Damnit. It has to be Vanessa Vaughn. His mood darkened further. Vanessa would recognize the buildings. She wasn't dumb. And she'd never shut up about it. He drove faster toward the Past (Eleanora) bypassing the detention center altogether. The judge hung up and made another call.

CHAPTER 37

THE DELUGE LASTED for nearly forty-five minutes. Trapped in the steamy car, Vanessa had talked while Terri sketched and the air conditioner had breathed feebly. In that time, Terri had created a hilariously illustrated organizational chart-cum-family tree. It connected the Whitney sisters and bank, Brinker's real estate company, Judge Montgomery, Commissioner Scotty Berens and the complicit County zoning commissioners, the Landmarks Board, and the Historical Society members to each of the properties Vanessa had identified in the Past.

"Shame on them. Shame, shame, shame," Vanessa said.

It was an audacious scam the judge and his despicable relatives had been running these past however many years. *God*, Terri thought. *This could have been going on for decades.*

In Palm Beach County, you didn't need to own a property to petition for its landmarking. They could target old buildings on valuable sites and landmark them intentionally to depress their value. Whenever the owners would apply for upgrade or expansion permits and variances they were denied out of hand, just like Terri had been denied the tent permit and the terraced room variance. Eventually these owners, not legally allowed to expand or upgrade their homes, would sell them for far below their market value. Then, once the judge and his toadies acquired the property, any landmark designation or building restrictions would magically disappear. Every accommodation could be made, up to and including carting the historic building off the property entirely.

"Twice during my tenure on the Historic Landmarks Board homes were relocated. If they were imperiled with coastal erosion, for example, an argument could be made. Keeping the old buildings intact was the priority."

"An exploitable priority," Terri added.

"One gentleman moved his beloved, historic home to Texas with him. He had his doctor claim it was necessary for his mental health, and he had the money to do it. But this? Who could have ever dreamed?" Vanessa said.

"Judge Montgomery. He dreamed. And those detestable clone sisters," Terri said.

"Dear, you have to start up here," Vanessa said, pointing across Terri at the top left of her drawing. It had developed into more comic book than organizational chart. It was sketched over the backs of several print-out pages. The Whitney sisters were depicted as a paper doll chain with bandit masks and holding cash bags, complete with $$$. The judge and Brinker were drawn Alfred Hitchcock-profile style, like chinless snowmen with hair. "It started with the gate to our path getting smashed. I know because I remember I met you the very next day," Vanessa said. "Draw that as a big bug spattered on a windshield."

"Okay," Terri said. "Way to get in the spirit." Vanessa was a lot more bloodthirsty than Terri gave her credit for. "But this is the pattern for all the buildings you've confirmed in the Past—not just Lola May's. This is the template for their crimes. Like—insert property here."

The late day sun burst through the clouds, and the rain stopped as quickly as it had began. A few vagrant types ventured outside of the dilapidated buildings and suspiciously eyed Terri and Vanessa in Terri's little car. Behind them, a giant, bald guy in a mechanic jumpsuit walked up to Terri's car as if he were going to open her trunk. Terri was watching this in blurry vision in her rearview mirror.

This isn't good. Terri didn't need Vanessa's coaching to spur her into action. She was already gassing it. Her back tires spun uselessly in the slick mud.

"Go, dear. Drive. Drive. He's reaching into his pocket. He's—he's—my God. He's got a gun. Drive, Terri. NOW. The man has a gun."

The back tires bit, and Terri drove. It started raining again, and they slid and bumped. Her little car barely sputtered forward. The guy behind her was easily keeping pace. Terri pushed the gas pedal to the floor, gained a little traction, and shot forward blindly. She had the feeling she was veering off the main track but couldn't see.

Vanessa had helpfully turned Terri's windshield wipers back on. They smeared a thick layer of mud across the glass as she shouted, "Faster, Terri. Faster. Oh—oh, he has a phone. It's not a gun. It's okay, dear, it's a phone."

Great, Vanessa. Now that I've had a stroke and destroyed my car, Terri thought. She was perfectly ill from the adrenalin rush. Terri slowed way down now that she wasn't fleeing for her life, but just as she came to a stop, there was a jolting *BAM.*

Terri's axle broke. It pitched Terri's car nose first into a ditch with a jolt. *BANG.* the airbags deployed. She and Vanessa were pitched into them.

"Fuck. I'm sorry, Mrs. Vaughn. Fuck." Terri said. They weren't hurt. Just surprised. As the air bags slowly deflated, their seat belts were they only thing keeping Vanessa and Terri from crashing into the dashboard. Despite the awkward angle, Vanessa Vaughn opened her purse and fished out an old flip phone. Terri didn't even know she owned a phone. And, apparently, service. *Oh, thank God.*

"Hello? Hello? This is Vanessa Vaughn. I'm trapped in a swamp, and I can't get out. I need immediate assistance—no, *you're garbled.* Speak slower." Vanessa listened, "Yes, yes, just put Captain Bradley on the line, hmm?"

CHAPTER 38

THE BIG, BALD guy in the mechanic's overalls relayed Terri and Vanessa's movements to Judge Montgomery.

"Yes, the women made it to the Past. Took the main route in. They got out of their car and looked around some. The babe took lots of pictures. The old one was all upset. Then the rain chased 'em off, but they didn't get far. Their car broke down—yeah, less than a half mile out."

"Son, you did fine. I have another matter. You get down to the gator preserve. The east gate. You know where that is?" the judge drawled. "Open it. It's on a timer. You bypass that timer. Open it. Then you skedaddle along. Understand?"

Montgomery hung up after his instructions were affirmed. He had stopped his big Bentley at the sign marked Drainage Canal 4-82. Above it, and partially hidden by foliage, was another sign. It was much larger and dirtier with "Everglades Rehabilitation and Detention Center" and the Florida State Seal underneath, and an arrow pointing to the right. Montgomery told Brinker to get out and fetch it. Disgruntled, Brinker shoved his bulk out of the car and squished through mud in his soft Italian loafers (they weren't nearly enough after the downpour, and his shoes were destroyed easily). Brinker flicked his hair and squished along until he reached the sign. He tugged it out of the ground, and he tossed it in the judge's trunk. He did this three more times, at drainage Canals 48-C, 49-C, and A-50. Then Brinker replaced the signs so those with right pointing arrows now pointed left, and vice-versa.

"We got one more stop, then we're riding up to Jupiter for some supper. Get my car detailed. Get you cleaned up, boy," the judge only called Brinker "boy" when he was mad, so Brinker shut up about how they had peons to change the signs and he shouldn't have had to ruin his shoes. He knew the drill. They'd done this before.

"You shoulda brought your damn boots, boy. You're filthy—and you don't have the sense God gave a goose."

A few minutes later, the judge rolled up to a stop before a large sign that read: "Danger: Alligator Preserve. Keep out." The judge and Brinker both got out of the car. They used box cutters to cut the huge metal sign down and then dragged if off to the side of the narrow, dirt road. They tried to bury it but mostly smeared mud over it. While they worked, they could hear the whir of the huge rolling gates to the alligator preserve grinding open, and they picked up their pace. The judge and Brinker hurled themselves back inside the car as soon as they finished their task.

The gator preserve was made of chain-link fencing on three sides: north, east, and south. The west side, like in the Past, was open to the Everglades. The north and south sides were fixed, while the east fence had a giant rolling gate that could be opened about forty feet. Now that the east gate was cranked open, the judge stepped on it as soon as he and Brinker got back in the car. He drove two miles before he stopped and called Sheriff Jones back with more specific instructions.

CHAPTER 39

AFTER PARKING HIS car in the reserved detectives lot and walking into the Everglades Rehabilitation and Detention Center, Detective E. Shay felt more exhausted and frustrated than he could remember being in a long time. He was getting nowhere on any of his cases,
and that was embarrassing. He knew everyone in the department
was a bit impressed with him: a genuine, hard-boiled Baltimore detective. They expected him to deliver. Surprisingly, E. Shay liked and
respected most of them in return, and he expected himself to deliver
too. So far, he was disgusted with himself.

Where the hell is Terri?

"Nice sky," Jill said perkily from behind her window. The front
desk sergeant at the center had been flirting with E. Shay since the
day he'd arrived. She was blown a lot of shit for it too, which E.
Shay appreciated. It kept the situation light and from becoming a
departmental thing, even though they'd started calling him P. Shay
for "Pretty." Shay had no interest in Jill, and he was sure she wasn't
serious either. E. Shay glanced back and saw the promise of one of
Florida's more spectacular sunsets and grunted.

"Who put a bee in your shorts?" Jill asked.

"Distracted. Sorry," E. Shay said, divesting himself of his weapons
and sliding them through the metal divider. Jill buzzed him in the
bullet-proof door.

While E. Shay was buzzing in, Sherriff Jones was buzzing out, all geared up and carrying a weapons duffle and an assault rifle. E. Shay wasn't a Jones fan. He particularly didn't like the confederate flag in the rear window of Jones's personal vehicle right above the "Trump Country" bumper sticker.

"Where's he headed?" E. Shay asked.

"Out to the gator preserve. Some issue. Jones is a crack shot," Jill said.

E. Shay had been out to the preserve once since he'd arrived. He'd never seen so many alligators outside of a horror movie. There were thousands of them, all sliding and writhing on top of each other. It gave him the creeps.

After he collected his weapons, he headed to the office that he shared with the other detectives at the center. About half the squad was on their way home. The rest, like E. Shay, were on a case. Or maybe stumped, like he was.

E. Shay sat down at a vacant desk and logged on to the computer there, but something was wrong. "Something's wrong," E. Shay announced at large.

"No shit, P. Shay," Detective Callecchio said. "It's quiet. No phones. They suspended cell service out here five minutes ago. Some Homeland Security drill. We're all on radio. But don't worry. The chatter will be unbearable within the hour."

An excellent time to buckle down, E. Shay thought. *No distractions or excuses. Take it from the beginning. Scroll back.* E. Shay brought up his original accident report and started from there. The driver of the van was a Mr. Merl Dosette. Last known address Eleanora, Florida, which wasn't far away. He remembered seeing the name on a map when he was acclimating himself to the area. At the time of his death, Merl was twenty-six and a junkie with a record. There was heroin and drug paraphernalia found in his van. The van had been stolen the week before. E. Shay forced himself to read the itemized contents of the van: one dollar, thirty seven cents in change. Two McDonalds French fry boxes. One plastic juice drink cap. Four blue painter's tarps. The list went on for three pages, including pictures that basically described garbage. E. Shay's eyes were crossing.

There was half an envelope with "uvan" scrawled across it. The beginning of the word had been torn away. E. Shay thought about this. Andalusian was the street that ended at the path between the May and Vaughn Estates. Maybe Merl was a terrible speller? E. Shay knew he was reaching but had nowhere else to go but reexamine every grain of evidence he had previously dismissed as irrelevant. He wondered for the zillionth time where Terri was.

CHAPTER 40

TERRI WAS UNSTRAPPING her seat belt and breaking her nose on the steering wheel. It was really broken. And it bled a lot. She tried to brace herself but underestimated the force of gravity. When the seat belt gave, Terri slammed into the dashboard. *Oww.*

There wasn't a choice. It had to be done. Vanessa's phone had cut out of service, Terri's phone had none, their lungs were compressing from hanging from their seat belts, and it was getting dark. Most importantly, Terri's car was sinking. They had front-axeled into a gulley and Terri's car was steadily flooding. Her pedals were almost under water. Terri twisted around, kneeling awkwardly on the dashboard to unstrap Vanessa. Terri was getting blood everywhere, but there was nothing she could do about it.

"Oof," Vanessa was heavier than she looked. She came down hard, then nimbly twisted herself about but couldn't open her door. "Are you okay?" Terri asked.

"Yes, dear, keep moving," Vanessa commanded. Terri almost laughed. She climbed out her own door and pulled Vanessa out after her. All Terri could think about in that moment was snakes, like lyrics you can't get out of your head.

Snake, snake, snake, snake, snake.

She tried to think of other things but couldn't. The sky was crimson swirled with a scattering of black thunder clouds. They were too deep into the woods to tell direction.

Why wasn't I ever a Girl Scout who could tell direction from moss? Terri thought.

They decided to follow their own car tracks back to where they'd gone wrong. Eventually, their tracks would intersect with the more traveled road, and they could walk home from there if they had to. Facts were, even if Palm Beach P.D. took Vanessa Vaughn's SOS phone call seriously, she'd only told them she was stuck in a swamp and couldn't get out before she lost cell service completely. How many swamps were there in Palm Beach County? And it was a ditch, not a swamp. Or a gully, but not a ditch? What did it matter? Terri was struggling to keep a grip.

She searched around inside her disabled car for the pair of plastic, knee-high rain boots that lived there for sea wall inspections. And crack houses with fire ants. Joel had worn them last. Terri found them and gave them to Vanessa, who had only one shoe left.

"Thank you, dear," Vanessa said graciously, like Terri had handed her a cup of tea in the drawing room. They trudged through the mud, frequently stumbling. They waded through water-filled swales up to their shins. The temperature had dropped with the short thunderstorm, but not enough. Now the jiggers and mosquitos were back in force, swarming over them. They loved the blood from Terri's nose bleed, and it was smeared over them both.

"I saw this in a movie once," Vanessa said as she scooped up a glob of mud and smeared it on Terri's face. "Hold still, dear. This will prevent these insidious little pests from eating us alive."

"Jesus, Vanessa, I can do it myself," Terri said, fighting Vanessa off.

"It's an excellent natural repellant." *So are you,* Terri thought, and then instantly regretted it. Vanessa had been a brick, considering. All

Terri had wanted to do was prove to Vanessa that *Casa Rosa* didn't have any roses on it. That's all. She should have left it at that—not gone racing out to the Past on some wild hunch, albeit a wild hunch that turned out to be true. Terri and Vanessa soldiered on side by side in the steamy, late afternoon.

"Hold your arms out like so, and you won't slip so much. Why do you think tightrope walkers walk thus? Hmm?"

"Thus? Really Vanessa? Thus?" Terri said and giggled—only a tiny bit hysterically.

Her nose hurt. Vanessa talked on. The sky deepened to a dark tangerine. They found where Terri had veered off and picked up the narrow dirt road they'd come in on. It was a little easier going but not much. It was wet and muddy and lumpy and slippery. They hadn't gone far when they came to the drainage canal sign that marked their turn.

Right. Left? Shit. Terri couldn't remember. *Was it Drainage Canal 48C that was a left turn? There were two lefts and two rights coming in. So reverse that? Shit, this is bad.*

It was going to be dark soon. Terri guessed they had forty minutes of daylight left, but a two hour walk ahead of them, especially if the terrain stayed this bad. Terri had no phone service and was saving her remaining battery life for flashlight mode. A bad decision here had serious consequences, and it was all Terri's fault.

Oh my God, I can't believe what a complete, selfish ass I am. Just to satisfy my own curiosity. Terri would never forgive herself if something happened to Mrs. Vaughn, though her incessant talking proved she was doing okay for now.

"What?" Terri said, hearing the tail end of Vanessa's sermon.

"The sign. To the detention center. It's this way, dear," Vanessa said, adding, "And don't stop. I may not restart." A few feet above the small, green canal marker was a rectangular sign to the detention center with an arrow painted on it. It was dirty and partially obscured, but there it was. Terri's semi-hysterical giggles burbled forth in overwhelming relief.

They hadn't noticed the sign driving in because they were searching for the low canal markers. Terri and Vanessa followed the arrow pointing back to the detention center arm in arm, slipping, stumbling, and splashing.

"The Palm Beach Police Department has no idea where we are, do they?" Vanessa asked.

"That's a hard no, Mrs. Vaughn. I'm so sorry for dragging you into this."

"Everyone needs a little excitement. A little rigorous activity never hurt anyone either. We shall hike however far we must until we reach civilization, hmm? Stand up straight, Terri; you're slouching."

They slogged onward until, relieved, they found the next sign.

"Don't stop, dear." Vanessa said.

"I have to re-mud," Terri said, now nearly shouting over the drone of a billion insects, who were vicious at sunset. Terri muddied herself, then did the same for Vanessa. They trudged on companionably, but increasingly uncomfortably. Terri knew the boots had to be giving Vanessa painful blisters. At least Terri's nose pain distracted her from other areas of bodily distress. It was throbbing with every jolting step, and she'd been breathing through her mouth since it happened. Protein wasn't an issue anymore. She'd inhaled a colony of bugs.

******

Sherriff Jones' geared up and headed out to the gator preserve as soon as he'd hung up with the judge. He took a forgotten farming track to reach a utility outpost on the southeast corner of the gator preserve. The outpost had an equipment shack where hoses, rakes, oil, tools, and general machine works were stored, and it housed another override for the eastern gator preserve gate. Sheriff Jones climbed to the roof of the shack, wearing full camouflaged attire.

He found Terri and Vanessa easily from his vantage point and watched their progress through his field glasses. Sherriff Jones squawked Judge Montgomery on the obscure radio frequency they'd decided on after Judge Montgomery had the cell service out there suspended. It crackled inside the Bentley. The judge had been idling just inside Canal Marker 40C, waiting for confirmation.

"Two people: small, slight builds, entering the gator preserve. They're covered in mud. Over," the sheriff squawked.

"Go on and close that gate. Let nature take its course. You hear me?" Judge Montgomery roared back. "But don't leave until it's done. Make sure. You know how. Over."

"Now can we go?" Brinker's wife, Beth Whitney Deeley, whined from the back seat.

"We should get as far away from here as possible. Not that we've done anything wrong. I mean, none of this has anything to do with us."

CHAPTER 41

THE CELL SERVICE suspension had so many radios crackling inside the detective's office at the detention center that E. Shay couldn't hear himself think. He tried to tune it out. Despite the volume, a few words crackled through.

"She said in a swamp." The radio crackled.

A swamp? Can't be. I'm not in Baltimore anymore, E. Shay thought and re-committed himself to ignoring the chatter and working. *Ha. Working? What a joke.* He knew he was bleeding to death from a thousand self-inflicted cuts. E. Shay's computer screen was filled with every scrap of information on and every photograph of Terri Somerville he could find. And E. Shay could find a lot. He knew all about that wanker first husband of hers and looked forward to punching the guy in the face—should the occasion arise—should Timothy ever return. But E. Shay would not let his personal feelings for Terri sway his investigation. He would go where the facts led.

"Oh, man, Pretty Shay has it bad." Detective Callecchio said, looking over E. Shay's shoulder at the screens full of Terri. "No one blames you, man. She was here today, like a ray of Florida sunshine."

"When? When today?" E. Shay asked.

"Maybe an hour before you," Callecchio said. "She wanted directions."

CHAPTER 42

IT WAS FULLY DARK outside, and Vanessa stopped.

"Dear, this feels terribly wrong to me. We should be seeing a twinkle of light in some direction by now, don't you think?" Vanessa asked.

"Methinks," Terri agreed, unhappily.

It was pitch black outside, and they hadn't used the phone flashlight feature yet to save battery power. But no one's night vision was this good. There was no moon, no stars, and they still had no cell service. It was time. Terri turned on the flashlight mode on her cell phone and scanned their surroundings. They stood in some sort of cleared, slippery area that looked like it had been trampled. A loud, grinding whir sound came from back the way they'd come.

Okay. That was good. Some sound of civilization. Maybe we should walk back toward it? Or run away from it? Terri didn't have a clue. And Vanessa had gone silent again. *Please, Vanessa don't fail me now. You've been a rock. I will kill myself if something happens to you.* The whirring stopped. Terri's flashlight beam just caught the end of a snake as it slithered over Terri's sneakered foot.

"Aiiiiiiiiiii." Terri blasted herself into space, screaming like a banshee. She clung to Vanessa and pranced, ridiculously, trying to keep her feet up off the ground. Vanessa slapped her. Hard. Terri was stunned. A red hand print bloomed across her face. She couldn't believe it. Vanessa had struck her. "Vanessa. That was so cliché." Terri burst out laughing. Then Vanessa burst out laughing too. They clung together in a little fit of nerves, laughing off the mounting tension, until Vanessa threatened to slap Terri again.

CHAPTER 43

WHAT THE BLOODY hell? E. Shay had missed getting T-boned by a whisker. A huge car barreled through the Everglades without its headlights on, doing forty—at least. Whatever it was had the greatest suspension E. Shay had ever seen. *Motherfucker.* Shay had to swerve off the road and into a ditch to avoid the crash. *Bastard*, E. Shay swore again, but he got the last four letters of the license plate and radioed it in.

UDGE

Now, he was stuck. His tires spun uselessly. Shay got out of the car, wedged some planks he had in his trunk under the back tires, and levered himself up and out of the quagmire. He was back on the road again heading toward the Past in less than five minutes. But he couldn't shake his escalating panic. He hit the gas hard and hoped his Dodge VX/hybrid was up to it. Out here in the glades, it felt like he was driving a lawn mower. E. Shay's high beams picked out where someone had detoured. Water still filled the tire tracks.

Would Terri detour off the main drag, way the hell out here in a marshy labyrinth? Of course she would, E. Shay concluded. *Because she's crazy.*

And he had lost his mind.

E. Shay followed the tracks that belonged to Terri's car. *Of course.* It was partially submerged. His heart crawled up in his throat. He approached the car and almost staggered with relief when he found it was empty, except for some general rubbish.

He shined his overpowered flashlight around the inside. There were a mess of colored pencils floating together, like rafted logs in the brake well. What looked like pages from a graphic novel were stuck to the seats and on the dashboard. Some pages were crumpled and torn. One bled into an abstract watercolor and was unreadable. But E. Shay saw enough to generally piece it together.

Holy shit.

He jogged back to his ride, got in, and slowly drove back to the turn off. He saw fresh footprints in the mud and slowed even more. He followed where they led while leaning out of the driver's open door with his high beams on. As soon as E. Shay saw the sign for the detention center, he knew it was pointing the wrong way. E. Shay had an infallible sense of direction. You could drop him in a well and he could orient himself to north, south, east, and west. It was an asset he was born with. He saw the footprints headed away from the detention center and farther into the glades. Just as he hit the gas, he thought he heard a scream.

CHAPTER 44

VANESSA'S SECOND SLAP had sobered Terri right up. A half-moon had risen and it was easier to see. They stood in what looked and felt like a rocky, muddy marsh. It was covered with slippery, crushed sawgrasses. Terri and Vanessa had gone wrong somewhere. *Damnit. Time to recalculate*, Terri decided and tried not to cry. Vanessa was handling this like a champ, and she was falling apart. *Buck up.*

And then Terri and Vanessa saw them at the same time, less than forty feet from where they stood. A thousand terrifying alligators. Huge and slimy, they lay in a giant, unmoving heap. Terri started trembling. Instinctively, she and Vanessa clung together and backed away as silently as possible. They tried to look like they weren't moving while they slowly inched backward, clutching each other tightly.

The gators began to wake. Giant ones. Baby ones. Green ones and black ones. They crawled and lumbered over themselves, punctuated by violent jaw snapping. At least six had developed an interest in Terri and Vanessa and had begun to slither toward them as they retreated.

"Vanessa, I'm so sorry. You're the greatest. I totally underestimated you. I'll never forgive myself for getting us killed," Terri said in a high-pitched rasp. Her throat closed in abject terror.

"Not US, I'm very hard to kill." Vanessa snapped. "Now, do something," she commanded.

Terri and Vanessa were backing up as fast as they could scurry. Thirty or more gators had joined the original six in pursuit. Terri flashed her phone light at them in desperation. It stopped them, blinding them for three or four seconds, but no more. Terri fumbled her phone and accidentally hit play. Taylor Swift shouted, "Shake it off. Shake it off."

Turns out alligators are not Taylor Swift fans.

The gators turned on themselves in a snapping frenzy that allowed Terri and Vanessa to put a few more valuable yards between them. *Give that girl another Grammy.* And then they came up against the fence and found the gate. Thank God. But it wasn't budging, no matter how hard they tugged and pushed and pulled.

Oh shit.

They bent over and put their backs to it with all their combined strength and might, but they couldn't find purchase on the slimy ground. The gate didn't budge. The alligators advanced.

Terri decided something. "Vanessa, you're going over." With adrenalin-spiked super-human strength and terror, she grabbed Vanessa and hoisted her up. She shoved Vanessa against the gate. "Step on my knee, then my shoulder." Terri instructed, straining under Vanessa's weight. "Oof."

Vanessa had kicked Terri right in the stomach, but it was okay. She had to hand it to Vanessa. She was game. She didn't bitch, and she didn't surrender. Vanessa shook off Terri's rubber boots and, using Terri and the gate for leverage, she clawed her way up. Terri knew Vanessa's fingers must be bloody and raw by now, clenching onto the chain links. Amazingly, their stacked, doubled size had frightened the gators into retreat. There was seventy-five feet between them.

"It's too high to scale, dear." Vanessa said. "I can't get over it."

"Then cling there," Terri growled, every muscle straining under

Vanessa's weight. She only outweighed Vanessa by ten pounds, and her shoulder was screaming under the strain.

The gators advanced again, with one huge male in the lead. Terri and Vanessa screeched and gestured as threateningly as possible without toppling themselves. Again, the gators retreated a few feet.

"How stupid do you think these alligators are?" Terri asked, wondering how long her shoulder would hold out.

"Not *that* stupid." Vanessa stood with one foot on Terri's shoulder and ten fingers and five toes death-gripping the chain-linked fence above Terri's head. "Come up here." She tried to transfer her weight off Terri's shoulder. The huge alligator was back, only moving faster this time. Terri shook so hard she was rattling the fence behind her. Terri tasted muddy sweat and blood and Chanel No. 5. Then, the giant alligator opened its massive jaws and lunged.

CHAPTER 45

SHERIFF JONES STOOD on top of the utility shack. He watched Terri and Vanessa and the alligators through the nightscope attached to his assault rifle. Mostly he watched Vanessa because she was on top. And the judge had made it clear. No one left the preserve. Jones couldn't be more pleased the woman was trying to climb over the fence and he could speed things along. Jones had had a long day. He wanted to go home and watch TV. When he finished with this, he still had to go get a tow rig and find the women's car. Then he had to tow it and dump it another three miles deeper into the glades. It'd take him another hour, at least, but no one would ever find it there. That was a fact.

Sherriff Jones looked through his scope and settled in for the shot. *I'll be damned. That old woman can climb like a monkey.* He changed his aim to Terri. He'd take her out from underneath the old bag. He wondered how long Vanessa could hold herself up without the other woman's support. Sherriff Jones steadied his breathing like his Pa, a card-carrying member of the NRA, taught him to do all those years ago. Then he fired.

BOOM.

****

E. Shay pushed his Dodge VX/hybrid to its limit. If he wasn't an inch shorter after this spine jarring ride he'd be surprised. He sped toward the scream he'd heard in growing alarm. From fifty feet away, E. Shay's headlights silhouetted Terri and Vanessa clinging to the gator preserve fence, one on top of the other. A massive gator was charging toward them. Shay leapt out of his car while it was still moving and saw the beast launch itself.

BOOM.

CHAPTER 46

BOOM.

THE HIGH-POWERED RIFLE report sounded like a dull thud from inside the car, and the judge gave a little chuckle.

"Now can we leave? Obviously, the situation's in hand, and I'm dying for a stiff drink," Beth Deeley said from the back seat. They had driven over to the Past to meet the huge bald guy in the mechanic's uniform who had reported on Terri's and Vanessa's movements. He materialized out of the Past when the big Bentley rolled up, and walked over to the driver's side to collect his pay. The judge shot him point blank through the open window of his Bentley. He'd used a silencer, even though he wasn't worried about being heard or about the cruiser he'd nearly rammed. No one patrolled way out here, except Sherriff Jones or Jones's men. The judge owned them all.

"I could use a drink myself," Judge Montgomery agreed.

****

BOOM.

The explosion was deafening. Vanessa screamed, and Terri felt her buckle above her. There was a scorching red everywhere and searing heat. Then nothing. Until now. Now the red pulsed painfully behind Terri's closed eyes, and she struggled to open them. She got them open a slit and the red flashed alternately blue. Back and forth, back and forth. The strobing light made Terri sick. She was lying on her back in the back seat of E. Shay's car with her head in Vanessa's lap and cotton balls up her nose. There was an annoying buzzing in Terri's ears.

"What?" Terri croaked out. Vanessa was holding insta-ice to Terri's forehead with heavily bandaged hands.

"Thank heavens you're back. What? I'll tell you what. Someone shot that, that behemoth. Then your detective, well, he was the most heroic. He tossed car flares everywhere and had the alligators in full retreat. And dear, I've never seen anyone cut open a fence so quickly. And there you were. Out cold. Limp as a sack of oats. Only leaking blood *everywhere*. The detective carried you the whole way here, you know."

Terri smiled a little dreamily and then remembered he'd confiscated her clothing after he'd slept with her—the pig.

Vanessa kept talking. "He was even gallant enough to offer to carry me. But I said 'No, thank you.' He gave me this medical kit and bandaged us both. You've bumped your head. You may have a concussion, dear. Hmm?"

CHAPTER 47

NO ONE SHOT the alligator. That gator hurled itself into the path of Jones's bullet. Jones was on top of the utility shack, aiming squarely at Terri. E. Shay was there. He saw Jones fire from the roof.

And Terri hadn't bumped her head. She got clocked with weaponized gator hide, thanks to the excessive force of Jones' assault rifle and a suicidal reptile. Terri was dead weight in E. Shay's arms and still unconscious when he'd left her with Mrs. Vaughn. He'd wanted to stay until the medics showed up, but he had crime scenes and evidence to secure. Detective Callecchio had arrived within minutes in an older, better version of E. Shay's car. Callecchio's was the loudest in a growing chorus of approaching sirens. After seeing the names on Terri's drawings, E. Shay had called out the cavalry. No way would he let these crimes get buried out here. He hopped in with Detective Callecchio, and they took off to find Terri's car. Plus the UDGE car.

And Sherriff Jones.

CHAPTER 48

IT HAD BEEN five days since Terri and Vanessa had discovered the Past for themselves, and Terri had been hiding out in her loft ever since. She had two black eyes, a swollen nose, fifteen stitches on her knee, and another twelve on her head. Everywhere else was black and blue or scratched and bitten raw.

Since she had no real estate license, she wasn't missing work and decided to hole up for a good sulk. It had taken the rest of that night to get patched up at the hospital—another huge expense Terri couldn't afford. And she found reporters camped outside her building when she got home. Apparently, news of Judge Montgomery's friends and family real estate program had broken. Terri ignored them and ran inside. She was poor and hurt, for God's sake. Why wouldn't anyone let her wallow in peace?

Terri refused to open her mail and turned her phones, TV, and wi-fi off. All of it. She lived on a box of dry Rice Krispies for two days before ordering in, and then only because she'd run out of Titos. She wouldn't answer her endlessly buzzing doorbell either. But Joel had his own key and showed up on day five.

"You look like shit," he asserted while nagging Terri into show-ering. Then he re-taped her head stitches to keep them dry and washed her hair for her in the kitchen sink because he couldn't bear it anymore. Joel rummaged through Terri's clothes and handed her what to wear.

"I'm not going anywhere," Terri protested, looking at the pretty dress he'd chosen.

"Oh, but you are," Joel countered. The story had grown to include so many Palm Beach bigwigs that Terri's and Vanessa's involvement was already out of the news cycle. The reporters had decamped.

"You have to go see Lola May. She's worried. And you need to air yourself."

"Air myself?" Terri made a face and sniffed herself, but she let Joel tug her to the elevator. "I have been through hell." Terri shouted in the car on the way.

"So blow me. Life goes on. Right now, everyone's worried about you. How selfish are you going to be?" Joel scolded. They pulled in front of Lola May's, and Joel told her to go in.

"Aren't I banned from here? Anthony will probably have me arrested," Terri argued but got out of the car. Joel drove off and left her.

"Hey. Seriously?"

Mrs. Irish had the door open. She looked Terri up and down and said, "Ach, ya poor lass. Come in with ya." This is why she didn't want to see anyone. She was too raw. It was all Terri could do to not burst into tears.

Lola was enthroned at the head of her dining table, gin in hand. Vanessa sat beside her.

Oh no. Terri wasn't ready to face Vanessa. She'd nearly killed the woman. By rights, Mrs. Vaughn could have pressed charges. And Terri had thought so many unkind things about Vanessa when she'd turned out to be so courageous and dear—in her own, overbearing way. Terri thought she was going to cry—but also thought this was weird.

What was Vanessa doing here, hanging out with Lola? She could see Lola teleporting herself away. Vanessa wasted no time.

"What I was saying when we got sidetracked with your *Casa Rosa* painting was you're going to have to write up a new contract for Lola May's. We had come to terms, you know. I'm buying it."

"What?" Terri said like a dunce.

"Dear, I'm buying it," Vanessa continued. "It only makes sense. Lola can lease it back. It ensures Herman's future—at a renegotiated price now, of course. And once it's disentangled from this landmarking fraud, we can have it properly reevaluated. You'll handle this for us, Hmm?"

"My real estate license was revoked."

"Not anymore. It's all been sorted out, dear. I have personally spoken with your Peepers fellows, the Virgas, and you have been reinstated."

Mrs. Irish returned with tea for Vanessa and a fresh pitcher of gin for Lola. She said, "Terri, that detective be at the front door for you. Again."

Terri felt an exquisite joy sear through her and then squashed it with all her might. *To hell with him.* Terri thought. His face was a mass of acne on her easel in her loft. She would concentrate on that. Terri had been 100% open and honest with him. She'd been *naked* with him. All while he thought she was a crazed murderer. *He can rot.* Terri wasn't going.

"Don't be ridiculous," Vanessa scoffed.

"Best see him, lass, or he'll just keep coming around," Mrs. Irish said, and she was literally tugging Terri up out of her chair.

Even Lola chimed, "Oh, do go on, sweetie. Stop fighting it. You're exhausting us all." And she unwound today's trailing gossamer scarf and handed it to Terri, vaguely motioning for her to wrap it around herself.

Terri didn't get what Lola was gesturing about until she met E. Shay outside.

CHAPTER 49

E. SHAY WINCED HARD when Terri stepped outside Lola's front door and he saw her battered face. He was holding her clothes and shoes in a clear, plastic evidence bag. He looked down.

Way to set the mood. "Your clothes," he said, offering the bag out to her. Terri was wrapping the scarf around her face and head like she was a cotton candy cone.

She stepped toward him to take the bag and saw he held a box of donuts too. "And what about those?" Terri wondered, taking the plastic bag. She was starving.

"For Herman," said E. Shay, before awkwardly asking Terri if she would walk with him to Herman's shed. "Please? Herman is worried about you too."

That's a really low request.

E. Shay knew Terri wouldn't hurt Herman's feelings. She walked with him, but only for Herman's sake. E. Shay stopped halfway there. He faced Terri with pleading eyes.

"Forgive me, Terri. I never meant to hurt you. I had to work this case with the facts and clues I had. That's my job. That you were caught in the crosshairs of these murderers still makes my blood run cold. And then your discovering and exposing this epic fraud I'm— I'm in awe of you." He said it with such sincerity Terri wanted to believe him.

"Not shock-and-awe?" Terri said sarcastically. Shay dropped the donuts on the ground and dug his way through the mile of scarf to find Terri's face. He took her in his arms.

"I'm not joking. I'm falling in love with you." he added angrily, and then he kissed her—carefully, at first, then with more *OOMPH.*

Terri's head spun and her knees buckled, and she clung to him just to remain standing. He was such a good kisser. Then Terri shoved herself away from him.

"Don't do that. You're stopping my thoughts," Terri shot back, breathless.

"I'm sorry. I have nothing but admiration for your thoughts," E. Shay said.

"You should. I'm the super sleuth here. I—I'm wearing my sleuth face. It comes in colors, and it's inflatable," Terri said.

"Well, sleuth face, what do you have to say about eleven hundred pounds of rotting, deceased house pets stolen from the Peaceful Pets Crematorium?" E. Shay asked and reached to take Terri's hand.

"Oh, I know. I know." Terri answered like a game show contestant. "A—a vulture hatchuary?" E. Shay burst out laughing. Terri continued, "I know. I have these, well, clients? They locked me out on a balcony."

THE END

30736638R00135

Made in the USA
Columbia, SC
29 October 2018